英汉对照典藏本

亚瑟王与圆桌骑士的故事
韵文罗曼史的经典之作

高文爵士与绿衣骑士

[英] 布莱恩·斯通 译
（现代英语译本）

陈才宇 译
（简体中文译本）

浙江工商大学出版社
·杭州·

图书在版编目（CIP）数据

高文爵士与绿衣骑士 /（英）布莱恩·斯通译；陈才宇
译. —杭州：浙江工商大学出版社，2019.1（2022.8 重印）

ISBN 978-7-5178-2893-8

Ⅰ.①高… Ⅱ.①布… ②陈… Ⅲ.①叙事诗－诗集－
英国－中世纪 Ⅳ.①I561.23

中国版本图书馆 CIP 数据核字（2018）第 184962 号

高文爵士与绿衣骑士
GAOWEN JUESHI YU LYUYI QISHI

[英]布莱恩·斯通 译

陈才宇 译

出 品 人	鲍观明
策划编辑	钟仲南
责任编辑	沈　娴
责任校对	姚　媛
封面设计	观止堂_未氓
责任印制	包建辉
出版发行	浙江工商大学出版社
	（杭州市教工路 198 号　邮政编码 310012）
	（E-mail：zjgsupress@163.com）
	（网址：http://www.zjgsupress.com）
	电话：0571-88904980,88831806（传真）
排　　版	杭州朝曦图文设计有限公司
印　　刷	杭州宏雅印刷有限公司
开　　本	880mm×1230mm　1/32
印　　张	8.125
字　　数	189 千
版 印 次	2019 年 1 月第 1 版　2022 年 8 月第 2 次印刷
书　　号	ISBN 978-7-5178-2893-8
定　　价	60.00 元

译　序

　　《高文爵士与绿衣骑士》(*Sir Gawain and the Green Knight*) 是英国罗曼史文学中最具艺术性的一部作品。虽然这首长篇叙事诗在题材上未能摆脱一般罗曼史作品表现骑士冒险的老套路，但其以无比深刻的象征意义和别致的艺术形式卓立于罗曼史文学之林，在英国早期文学史上占据显著的地位。

　　原稿用英国北部方言，即南兰开夏地区的方言写成，收在《卡顿抄稿集》中，藏于大英图书馆。诗的作者一直是个谜。对此有几种说法：一种说法认为，根据它与另一首题为《珍珠》的罗曼史在写作风格上存在某些相似之处，作者可能是约翰·多恩(John Donne)或约翰·普拉特(John Prat)；第二种说法称作者是15世纪的罗曼史作家胡乔恩(Huchown)；第三种说法则言作者为牛津一位名叫拉尔夫·斯特罗德(Ralph Strode)的学者。这几种说法都不成定论。在没有更充分的材料被发现以前，作者问题只能悬着。文学史的描述中，一般用"《高文爵士与绿衣骑士》作者"称之。

　　这首罗曼史讲的是砍头不死的神话：绿衣骑士在某年的圣诞节前来挑战圆桌骑士，亚瑟王(King Arthur)的侄子高文(Gawain)上前砍下了绿衣骑士的头颅。无头的绿衣骑士抢回自己的头颅，要求高文一年后去绿色教堂找他，接受他的回砍。次年，高文爵士践约，启程去寻找绿色教堂。圣诞节前投宿在一座城堡。城堡主外出打猎，高文在

1

城堡内受到女主人的百般诱惑而不为所动。之后在绿色教堂附近的丛林中,城堡主(即绿衣骑士)朝他连举三斧,没砍下他的头颅,只让他受了轻伤。高文回到亚瑟王的宫廷,大家都认为他的行为高尚纯洁,给圆桌骑士带来了光荣。

全部情节中,最不可思议的是砍头不死。早在八九世纪的爱尔兰史诗《逃亡的布里卡莱特》(又称《布里修的宴会》)中,就有关于砍头比武的描写:太阳神居丘莱恩(Cuchulain)与恐怖神乌斯(Uath)比试砍头。居丘莱恩让乌斯砍了三次,都毫发无伤。这个民间神话故事什么时候从爱尔兰传到英格兰和苏格兰,我们不得而知,但《高文爵士与绿衣骑士》的作者在创作这首罗曼史时对这个神话传说有所借鉴,这一点是肯定的。

太阳神居丘莱恩有一头美丽的金发,他的父亲是霞光之神卢格(Lug)。威尔士民间传说中也有一位金发天神,其名是高莱·高尔特林(Gwri Gwallterin),后来演变成高尔居梅(Gwalchmai),据说就是威尔士的高文。在亚瑟王及圆桌骑士的故事流传以前,这个神就已经存在了。据有关学者考证,"高尔居梅"的含义是"五月之鹰",而鹰在民俗中就是象征太阳的神鸟。在罗曼史中,诗人描写高文爵士的衣着打扮时,喜欢用"光彩夺目"一类的形容词,显然也暗示了其神性的一面。在圆桌骑士中,高文是仅次于亚瑟王的重要人物,论武艺虽不及朗斯洛(Lancelot),但以品德高尚著称。在早期罗曼史作品中,亚瑟王所佩带的那把能发光的神剑就归高文所有。在寻找圣杯的传说中,有一说法是高文最终到达了目的地,其他骑士都因自身的品德缺陷未能见到圣杯。

如果说高文隐喻太阳神居丘莱恩,那么,绿衣骑士就是恐怖神乌斯的化身。一开始,绿衣骑士就以超自然的形象出现:全身着绿,还有一头绿发,性情高傲、蛮横,被人砍下头颅而不死。非人性的凶神形象是他本质的一面;偶尔表现出来的人性的一面是他假装的,非本质的。绿色固然是生命力旺盛的表现,但这不是诗人要赞美的。绿色在绿衣骑士身上不能简单地联系到春天、青春和美好,而是象征荒野、死亡、鬼魂和罪恶。绿衣骑士有意安排自己的妻子去勾引高文,就像潜入伊甸园的蛇去诱惑夏娃和亚当,从这个意义上说,他就是魔鬼的化身。值得注意的还有他手中的武器,那不是中世纪骑士惯用的剑,而是斧。斧在中世纪的英国是挪威入侵者使用的武器,作者有意让绿衣骑士随身携带这样的凶器,是在强调斧的持有者的野蛮的、非理性的、非道德的和反文明的特质。

那位与丈夫共谋引诱高文的城堡女主人在诗中一直没有透露姓名,但种种迹象表明,她应该就是罗曼史中的妖仙摩根(Morgan)的化身。根据12世纪威尔士作家坎姆勃伦塞斯(Cambrensis)的意见,摩根象征的是爱尔兰战争女神摩利姑(Morrigu),她曾用自己的魔法反对太阳神居丘莱恩。再往前追溯,凯尔特人的女神玛特罗娜(Matrona)应该与她也有些关系。在北部意大利和莱茵河一带,流传着美人鱼引诱渔民上当,然后在拥抱中将其扼杀的传说,那个女妖的名字就是摩根。在罗曼史作品中,摩根成了亚瑟王的亲姐姐。王后奎妮佛(Guinevere)与湖上的朗斯洛通奸,被摩根发现;摩根让亚瑟喝了具有魔力的酒,得以目睹妻子的背叛行为。罗曼史中还有一种说法:摩根与骑士通奸,受到王后的揭发,导致被流放。摩根从此恨透了王后乃至整个文明世界。为了报仇,她拜魔法大师梅林(Merlin)为师,学得许多魔法,隐居于某峡谷的一座教堂中。凡是对爱情不专的人进入教堂,就别想活着出来。《高文爵士与绿衣骑士》中描写的那所小教堂,应该就是她的隐居地。

从上述考察可以看出，罗曼史故事的发生和演变与民间神话传说息息相关。作为一种文学现象，罗曼史是从民间神话传说演变而来。我国的批评界以往评价罗曼史时，总是过多地指责它的荒谬性。如果能从神话学的角度来看待这些"荒诞不经"的作品，并把它们看作神话的余墨，或者是神话传说向现实主义文学过渡的产物时，我们的批评就会变得宽容些。

《高文爵士与绿衣骑士》所蕴含的意义，即作者的最初构思，其实用心良苦。作者要告诉读者的是：高文爵士与绿衣骑士之间的对抗，意味着基督教的文明与异教的野蛮之间的对抗，或者说封建的秩序与原始社会形态的非秩序之间的对抗。高文爵士接受绿衣骑士的挑战，表现了他的勇敢；他践约前往绿色教堂，证明他是一个信守诺言的人；城堡女主人百般诱惑，他不为所动，则表现了其道德的纯洁性。女主人赠送高文以腰带，并非因为爱高文，而是为了加害于他。高文始终不为美色所惑，罗曼史的作者通过这件事不仅赞美了高文，还宣扬了教会的禁欲主义：情欲是死亡的象征，只有永葆道德纯洁的人，才能永远立于不败之地。

然而，作者在最后一天的试探中又让高文犯了一个小小的错误：接受女主人的腰带而不守约将它交出。这个错误导致他受了轻伤。意味深长的是，这条证明高文的错误的腰带被带回亚瑟王的宫廷时，圆桌骑士们一致视之为美德与荣誉的象征。罗曼史的作者有意进行这样的描写，是对世俗观念的一种让步。人无完人，应该允许人性中存在缺陷。稍有瑕疵的美德已是人类能达到的最高境界。《高文爵士与绿衣骑士》以貌似荒唐的情节给了我们一个富有哲理的启示：完美的行为准则与人性的局限之间，始终存在着一定的距离。

在艺术表现上，这首罗曼史最突出的地方是巧妙地运用了对比、平衡和象征等艺术手法。尤其是象征的手法，被作者运用得炉火纯青，几乎不露痕迹。

绿色象征死亡、野蛮、情欲和罪恶。女主人的腰带象征世俗生活。这两个重要象征维系着作品的主题。此外，还有五角星的象征：中世纪的罗曼史作品中，骑士的徽章一般采用狮、鹰或鹰头狮身的神兽作为图案，而高文的盾牌上却是一个五角星（pentangle）。按照神秘教义的解释，pentangle一词是上帝耶和华的忌讳。还有一种说法：五角星最初是所罗门所设计的，用来表示神圣的真理，据说还有防范疾病和妖魔的功效。

还有城堡男主人狩猎所得的三只野兽，那也是有象征意义的：鹿、野猪和狐狸，分别代表肉体、恶魔和尘世。罗曼史研究专家布莱恩·斯通（Brian Stone）就认可这种说法。中世纪的雕刻中，经常能见到这三只野兽的图案。教堂中至今还保存着画有这种图案的洗礼盘。斯顿说他在自己的家乡就见过这种洗礼盘，上面画着一只凶猛的野猪，正张牙舞爪地用嘴拱着一棵代表神意的葡萄藤。

总之，象征手法的运用深化了诗歌的主题。甚至可以说，《高文爵士和绿衣骑士》全部的思想意义，都是通过象征手法体现的。

我的翻译依据1974年在伦敦出版的"企鹅经典丛书"（Penguin Classics）中的 *Sir Gawain and the Green Knight*（2nd ed.）。这是一个现代英语的译本，译者是中古英语文学专家布莱恩·斯通。

陈才宇

2018年5月5日于杭州寓所

CONTENTS/目录

Sir Gawain

高文爵士

By Howard Pyle

霍华德·派尔 绘

FIT I

1

THE siege and the assault being ceased at Troy,

The battlements broken down and burnt to brands and ashes,

The treacherous trickster whose treasons there flourished

Was famed for his falsehood, the foulest on earth.

Aeneas the noble and his knightly kin

Then conquered kingdoms, and kept in their hand

Wellnigh all the wealth of the western lands.

Royal Romulus to Rome first turned,

Set up the city in splendid pomp,

Then named her with his own name, which now she still has:

Ticius founded Tuscany, townships raising,

Longbeard in Lombardy lifted up homes,

And far over the French flood Felix Brutus

On many spacious slopes set Britain with joy

      And grace;

    Where war and feud and wonder

第一章

1

围攻特洛伊的战火已经熄灭，
城墙倒塌，烧成一片废墟，
背信弃义的骗子手得逞一时，
不忠的行径反使他们[1]声名卓著。
高贵的埃涅阿斯及其勇武的家族，
后来将诸多王国一一征服，
几乎夺取西部地区全部财富。
罗穆路斯最先返回罗马，
把那座城建造得雄伟壮丽，
他以自己的名字给它命名，并沿袭至今：
堤修斯建立图斯卡尼[2]，村镇拔地而起，
伦巴德在伦巴第[3]安家立业，
在与法国遥遥相望的大海彼岸
菲勒克斯·布鲁图斯[4]在群山上，以喜悦和恩典
　　创建不列颠，

　　战争、血仇和奇迹，

Have ruled the realm a space,

And after, bliss and blunder

By turns have run their race.

2

AND when this Britain was built by this brave noble,

Here bold men bred, in battle exulting,

Stirrers of trouble in turbulent times.

Here many a marvel, more than in other lands,

Has befallen by fortune since that far time.

But of all who abode here of Britain's kings,

Arthur was highest in honour, as I have heard;

So I intend to tell you of a true wonder,

Which many folk mention as a manifest marvel,

A happening eminent among Arthur's adventures.

Listen to my lay but a little while:

Straightway shall I speak it, in city as I heard it,

With tongue;

As scribes have set it duly

In the lore of the land so long,

With letters linking truly

In story bold and strong.

曾经充斥这片国土，
紧接着欢乐与悲戚，
轮番降临这个民族。

2

当这英武的贵胄创建不列颠，
骁勇之士便踊跃于沙场，
是非之徒一个个成了混世魔王。
从此以后，世上少见的许多奇迹，
一次次发生在这片土地上。
据我所知，在不列颠诸王中，
要数亚瑟王的名望最高；
因此我要给大家讲一个故事，
它是亚瑟冒险中一段经历，
许多人觉得它真实可信。
请诸位这就听一听我唱的歌，
这歌我从城里听来，在此将一一
　　　　如实转述；
　　　　就像执笔的抄稿员
　　　　将历史传说如实记述，
　　　　他用文字拼缀成篇，
　　　　使故事显得凿凿有据。

3

THIS king lay at Camelot one Christmastide
With many mighty lords, manly liegemen,
Members rightly reckoned of the Round Table,
In splendid celebration, seemly and carefree.
There tussling in tournament time and again
Jousted in jollity these gentle knights,
Then in court carnival sang catches and danced;
For fifteen days the feasting there was full in like measure
With all the meat and merry-making men could devise,
Gladly ringing glee, glorious to hear,
A noble din by day, dancing at night!
All was happiness in the height in halls and chambers
For lords and their ladies, delectable joy.
With all delights on earth they housed there together,
Saving Christ's self, the most celebrated knights,
The loveliest ladies to live in all time,
And the comeliest king ever to keep court.
For this fine fellowship was in its fair prime
   Far famed,
  Stood well in heaven's will,
  Its high-souled king acclaimed:

3

话说当年亚瑟在凯姆洛特[5]欢庆圣诞节，

他身边有众多气宇非凡的臣僚，

还有那班有资格列席圆桌的骑士，

人人体面而高雅，快活而逍遥。

高贵的骑士一次次相互角力，

在欢乐的气氛中比武争强，

随后又在宫廷里尽情跳舞歌唱。

宴席上山珍海味品尝不尽，

快活的艺人尽其所长献技助兴，

欢声笑语闻之心旷神怡，

喧腾狂欢持续了整整十五天。

厅堂楼台处处洋溢欢乐，

男男女女个个喜气洋洋。

人间英雄豪杰济济一堂：

著名的骑士、美艳的女子，

贤明的君主治国有方，

只差基督本人没有到场。

这次聚会真可谓盛况空前，

　　　遐迩闻名，

　　亚瑟王心灵高尚，

　　他说话代表了天意：

So hardy a host on hill

Could not with ease be named.

4

THE year being so young that yester-even saw its birth,

That day double on the dais were the diners served.

Mass sung and service ended, straight from the chapel

The King and his company came into hall.

Called on with cries from clergy and laity,

Noël was newly announced, named time and again.

Then lords and ladies leaped forth, largesse distributing,

Offered New Year gifts in high voices, handed them out,

Bustling and bantering about these offerings.

Ladies laughed full loudly, though losing their wealth,

And he that won was not woeful, you may well believe.

All this merriment they made until meal time.

Then in progress to their places they passed after washing,

In authorized order, the high-ranking first;

With glorious Guinevere, gay in the midst,

On the princely platform with its precious hangings

Of splendid silk at the sides, a state over her

Of rich tapestry of Toulouse and Turkestan

Brilliantly embroidered with the best gems

众豪杰会聚山上，

如何定名倒不容易。

4

幼稚的新年刚于昨晚降临，

第二天客人们在厅堂受到款待。

弥撒曲唱过，祷告仪式也已结束，

国王和他的骑士从教堂径直来到大厅。

随着僧侣和俗人的阵阵呼喊，

圣诞歌唱了一遍又一遍。

骑士和淑女们跑上跑下，

喧哗中把新年的礼物分发，

大伙儿围着这些礼物谈笑取乐。

女士们虽破费了钱财，但笑得开心，

得到礼物的男子当然不会不高兴。

就这样，大家一直嬉闹到宴席开始，

然后尊者在前，各按名分，

井然有序地回到自己的位置。

庄严的厅堂四周挂着珍贵的锦绣，

奎妮佛被众人簇拥在中间，

她容光焕发，喜色满面，

身上穿着图卢兹和突厥斯坦[6]的绫罗，

上面镶嵌着各种珍贵宝石，

Of warranted worth that wealth at any time

    Could buy.

    Fairest of form was this queen,

    Glinting and grey of eye;

    No man could say he had seen

    A lovelier, but with a lie.

5

BUT Arthur would not eat until all were served.

He was charming and cheerful, child-like and gay,

And loving active life, little did he favour

Lying down for long or lolling on a seat,

So robust his young blood and his beating brain.

Still, he was stirred now by something else:

His noble announcement that he never would eat

On such a fair feast-day till informed in full

Of some unusual adventrue, as yet untold,

Of some momentous marvel that he might believe,

About ancestors, or arms, or other high theme;

Or till a stranger should seek out a strong knight of his,

To join with him in jousting, in jeopardy to lay

Life against life, each allowing the other

The favour of Fortune, the fairer lot.

无论何时何地,钱物买不到
　　这一身装束。
　　王后风姿绰约无双,
　　一对黑眸光彩照人,
　　只要男人们不说谎,
　　此等丽姝天下难寻。

5

亚瑟王坚持让别人先入席。
他这人富有魅力,如孩子般无忧无虑,
他热爱热闹的生活,从来不贪睡,
很少见他身靠椅子养神将息。
他有一腔热血、好动的脑筋。
这回他胸中就涌动着一股激情,
在这喜庆的日子,他庄严宣布:
进餐以前,他要先听大家谈谈,
那些至今不为人知的历险,
那些有关祖先和战争的故事,
以及其他意义重大的人间奇迹。
要么他要先看看有谁会来挑战,
与他的骑士当场比试武艺,
在以生命对抗的冒险中,
让更公正的命运之神为他们裁决。

Such was the King's custom when he kept court,
At every fine feast among his free retinue

> In hall.

> So he throve amid the throng,

> A ruler royal and tall,

> Still standing staunch and strong,

> And young like the year withal.

6

ERECT stood the strong King, stately of mien,
Trifling time with talk before the topmost table.
Good Gawain was placed at Guinevere's side,
And Agravain of the Hard Hand sat on the other side,
Both the King's sister's sons, staunchest of knights.
Above, Bishop Baldwin began the board,
And Ywain, Urien's son ate next to him.
These were disposed on the dais and with dignity served,
And many mighty men next, marshalled at side tables.
Then the first course came in with such cracking of trumpets,
(Whence bright bedecked blazons in banners hung)
Such din of drumming and a deal of fine piping,
Such wild warbles whelming and echoing
That hearts were uplifted high at the strains.

自从他登基为王，每逢节庆日，
这种比武竞技的壮举早已——
　　　相沿成习。
　　在这班骑士中间，
　　国王显得格外高大，
　　他既坚毅又强健，
　　犹如新年生机勃发。

6

强健的国王站在圆桌前，
风度翩翩地与大家说话，
善良的高文坐在奎妮佛的一侧，
旁边是哈德汉的阿格雷范，
他俩都是国王的外甥、勇敢的骑士。
上首坐着主教贝尔德温，
他身边是尤里之子雨文。
这几位居上席备受尊敬，
其余要人分坐在他们两侧。
随着喇叭吹奏，第一道菜端上，
（喇叭上装饰着鲜艳的彩旗）
鼓声、笛声顿时响成一片，
激昂且悠扬的乐声回荡在整个大厅，
点燃了每个宾客的激情。

Then delicacies and dainties were delivered to the guests,

Fresh food in foison, such freight of full dishes

That space was scarce at the social tables

For the several soups set before them in silver

      On the cloth.

    Each feaster made free with the fare,

    Took lightly and nothing loth;

    Twelve plates were for every pair,

    Good beer and bright wine both.

7

OF their meal I shall mention no more just now,

For it is evident to all that ample was served;

Now another noise, quite new, neared suddenly,

Likely to allow the liege lord to eat;

For barely had the blast of trump abated one minute

And the first course in the court been courteously served,

When there heaved in at the hall door an awesome fellow

Who in height outstripped all earthly men.

From throat to thigh he was so thickset and square,

His loins and limbs were so long and so great,

That he was half a giant on earth, I believe;

Yet mainly and most of all a man he seemed,

美味佳肴传递到他们面前，
这些食物营养丰富，花式多样，
把一张张桌子摆得满目琳琅，
台布上更有几个银盘，里面盛着——
　　　鲜美的羹汤。
　　众宾客品尝着佳肴，
　　自由自在其乐融融；
　　每两人供菜十二道，
　　更有那啤酒葡萄酒。

7

关于酒宴我在此不再多言，
满桌美味佳肴盛况足见；
这时，突然响起一阵嘈杂声，
亚瑟王说过的话似乎已应验；
喇叭刚刚停止吹奏，
头道菜端上桌不久，
一个可怖的人物门口出现，
他比凡人高出一头。
从脖子到大腿结实健壮，
腰身与四肢既粗又长，
我相信，他有一半属于魔怪；
只是外表仍是凡人模样，

And the handsomest of horsemen, though huge, at that;

For though at back and at breast his body was broad,

His hips and haunches were elegant and small,

And perfectly proportioned were all parts of the man,

As seen.

Men gaped at the hue of him

Ingrained in garb and mien,

A fellow fiercely grim,

And all a glittering green.

8

AND garments of green girt the fellow about—

A two-third length tunic, tight at the waist,

A comely cloak on top, accomplished with lining

Of the finest fur to be found, made of one piece,

Marvellous fur-trimmed material, with matching hood

Lying back from his locks and laid on his shoulders;

Fitly held-up hose, in hue the same green,

That was caught at the calf, with clinking spurs beneath

Of bright gold on bases of embroidered silk,

But no iron shoe armoured that horseman's feet.

And verily his vesture was all vivid green,

So were the bars on his belt and the brilliants set

身材伟岸,作为骑士倒是仪表堂堂,

胸脯和脊背极其宽厚,

臀部和下腰匀称得当,

各个部位的比例真可谓

　　　完美无缺。

　　他那副装束和风采,

　　令大伙儿诧异万分,

　　好一个冷酷的汉子,

　　浑身上下绿光森森!

8

这家伙一身着绿装,

束腰外衣套住身体大半,

斗篷盖头,整块毛皮作衬里,

那毛皮可谓稀世珍异。

一条毛皮镶边的头巾,

从发际一直披到两肩,

下身穿一身同样绿色的紧身裤,

脚踝上绑着金制马刺一副,

在丝织垫子上叮当作响,

而战靴却没穿在脚上。

他全身上下穿戴成鲜绿色,

绿色的装备、绿色的丝绸马鞍,

In ravishing array on the rich accoutrements

About himself and his saddle on silken work.

It would be tedious to tell a tithe of the trifles

Embossed and embroidered, such as birds and flies,

In gay green gauds, with gold everywhere.

The breast-hangings of the horse, its haughty crupper,

The enamelled knobs and nails on its bridle,

And the stirrups that he stood on, were all stained with the same;

So were the splendid saddle-skirts and bows

That ever glimmered and glinted with their green stones.

The steed that he spurred on was similar in hue

> To the sight,

> Green and huge of grain,

> Mettlesome in might

> And brusque with bit and rein—

> A steed to serve that knight!

9

YES, garbed all in green was the gallant rider,

And the hair of his head was the same hue as his horse,

And floated finely like a fan round his shoulders;

And a great bushy beard on his breast flowing down,

With the heavy hair hanging from his head,

就连盛装上的带扣和宝石，
也一律采用绿色装饰。
那里面金子随处可见，
但刺绣其上的虫鸟图案，
细细叙说就不免厌烦，
再说那马身上的披挂，
包括胸饰、兜带、缰辔与马镫，
也都用绿色的颜料染成；
此外还有整副绿色的鞍鞴，
绿色的宝石在那里忽闪忽闪，
就是他的骏马也是同样颜色。

  在人面前，
  这匹绿马何其高大，
  英姿飒爽，健壮无比，
  马嚼子与缰绳制不住它，
  天生是骑士的坐骑!

9

不错，骁勇的骑士全身披绿，
就连头上毛发也与坐骑同色，
像一叶扇垂挂在肩膀；
浓密的胡子在胸前飘拂，
那沉沉的毛发从头上披下，

Was shorn below the shoulder, sheared right round,
So that half his arms were under the encircling hair,
Covered as by a king's cape, that closes at the neck.
The mane of that mighty horse, much like the beard,
Well crisped and combed, was copiously plaited
With twists of twining gold, twinkling in the green,
First a green gossamer, a golden one next.
His flowing tail and forelock followed suit,
And both were bound with bands of bright green,
Ornamented to the end with exquisite stones,
While a thong running through them threaded on high
Many bright golden bells, burnished and ringing.
Such a horse, such a horseman, in the whole wide world
Was never seen or observed by those assembled before,
  Not one.
  Lightning-like he seemed
  And swift to strike and stun.
  His dreadful blows, men deemed,
  Once dealt, meant death was done.

10

YET hauberk and helmet had he none,
Nor plastron nor plate-armour proper to combat,

20

在肩膀下剪平,形成一圈,
半条手臂已埋在那下面,
毛发上还盖着披巾,紧靠脖颈。
骏马的鬃毛也与胡子相似,
卷曲有致,编成一根根辫子,
束束鬃毛间夹着缕缕金丝,
在绿色的背景下闪耀。
飘动的马尾和额毛也一式一样,
都用耀眼的绿带作为套环,
端处一概饰以精致的宝石,
皮鞭则高横在马背上,
许多闪光的铃铛在那里叮当作响。
如此的骏马,如此的骑手,
普天下任何地方找遍,

  也难得一见。

  就像闪电划过长空,

  他的手段神速非常,

  有谁一旦被他击中,

  死亡即降临他身上。

10

但他没有穿锁子甲,没戴头盔,
未着胸铠和其他适合战斗的装备,

Nor shield for shoving, nor sharp spear for lunging;

But he held a holly cluster in one hand, holly

That is greenest when groves are gaunt and bare,

And an axe in his other hand, huge and monstrous,

A hideous helmet-smasher for anyone to tell of;

The head of that axe was an ell-rod long.

Of green hammered gold and steel was the socket,

And the blade was burnished bright, with a broad edge,

Acutely honed for cutting, as keenest razors are.

The grim man gripped it by its great stong handle,

Which was wound with iron all the way to the end,

And graven in green with graceful designs.

A cord curved round it, was caught at the head,

Then hitched to the haft at intervals in loops,

With costly tassels attached thereto in plenty

On bosses of bright green embroidered richly.

In he rode, and up the hall, this man,

Driving towards the high dais, dreading no danger.

He gave no one a greeting, but glared over all.

His opening utterance was, 'Who and where

Is the governor of this gathering? Gladly would I

Behold him with my eyes and have speech with him.'

   He frowned;

  Took note of every knight

  As he ramped and rode around;

更没有防身的盾和拼杀的矛，
手上只握着一串圣洁的冬青，
此物经霜雪绿叶犹存，
另一只手提一把可怖的大斧，
那是令人厌恶的砍头武器，
斧刃的长度足有一厄尔[7]，
承口则用金子和钢铁打成，
宽阔的斧面磨得闪闪发光，
割物犹如剃刀般锋利非常。
这凶人将大斧提在手上，
那斧柄从上到下用铁皮包裹，
上面雕着优美的绿色图案。
斧柄上还绕着一根丝带，
中间有数处装饰着扣环，
上面垂挂着一串串流苏，
绿色的刺绣晶莹闪亮。
这家伙骑马进入大厅，
有恃无恐来到高台前。
他怒视众人，对谁也不打招呼，
开口就问："你们这次聚宴，
谁是主人？他在哪里？
我很想见见，有话说给他听。"
　　他皱着眉头，
　　骑马绕场奔走一周，
　　将众骑士一一端详，

Then stopped to study who might
Be the noble most renowned.

THE assembled folk stared, long scanning the fellow,
For all men marvelled what it might mean
That a horseman and his horse should have such a colour
As to grow green as grass, and greener yet, it seemed,
More gaudily glowing than green enamel on gold.
Those standing studied him and sidled towards him
With all the world's wonder as to what he would do.
For astonishing sights they had seen, but such a one never;
Therefore a phantom from Fairyland the folk there deemed him.
So even the doughty were daunted and dared not reply,
All sitting stock-still, astounded by his voice.
Throughout the high hall was a hush like death;
Suddenly as if all had slipped into sleep, their voices were
        At rest;
    Hushed not wholly for fear,
    But some at honour's behest;
    But let him whom all revere
    Greet that gruesome guest.

然后勒住骏马审究，
想弄清谁最得众望。

11

大伙儿久久注视着这位骑士，
人人对发生的事感到诧异非常，
为何骑手和坐骑这般模样！
那颜色竟与绿草匹配相当，
闪烁犹如金子上摆着绿珐琅！
站着的人[8]望着他，侧身向前，
他们怀着好奇心，想知道个究竟。
虽然见多识广，此事却头一遭碰上，
大家都当他是魔鬼来自仙乡；
即使胆大的也害怕得不敢出声，
大家站着不动，被他的声音震慑。
整个大厅变得死一般寂静，
一时间，似乎一切都进入睡眠，

　　　无声无息；

　　　但并非人人怕得发抖，
　　　有的是出于尊重他人，
　　　他们要让尊者先开口，
　　　让他迎接可怖的来宾。

12

FOR Arthur sendsed an exploit before the high dais,

And accorded him courteous greeting, no craven he,

Saying to him, "Sir knight, you are certainly welcome.

I am head of this house: Arthur is my name.

Please deign to dismount and dwell with us

Till you impart your purpose, at a proper time."

"May he that sits in heaven help me," said the knight,

"But my intention was not to tarry in this turreted hall.

But as your reputation, royal sir, is raised up so high,

And your castle and cavaliers are accounted the best,

The mightiest of mail-clad men in mounted fighting,

The most warlike, the worthiest the world has bred,

Most valiant to vie with in virile contests,

And as chivalry is shown here, so I am assured,

At this time, I tell you, that has attracted me here.

By this branch that I bear, you may be certain

That I proceed in peace, no peril seeking;

For had I fared forth in fighting gear,

My hauberk and helmet, both at home now,

My shield and sharp spear, all shining bright,

And other weapons to wield, I would have brought;

12

亚瑟感到历险建功的机会就在眼前，
他不是懦夫，懂得以礼相迎，
他说："足下，热烈欢迎你，
我是这里的首领，亚瑟是我名，
请屈尊下马与我们坐在一起，
直到时机合适通报此行目的。"
"愿在天的主帮助我，"骑士说，
"我无意在这座塔楼逗留，
阁下，你的声名响彻云霄，
你的城堡和骑士天下最好，
马上披挂作战，你的人最强大，
世上数你的人最好战、最高尚，
男子汉比武争胜，你的人最勇敢，
我相信，此处体现骑士的精神，
告诉你吧，就是这个把我吸引。
但请你放心，这枝冬青可以做证，
我要和平对垒，不求冒险。
如果我特意前来挑战，
我那留在家中的锁子甲和头盔，
那金光闪闪的盾和锋利的矛，
以及其他武器，就一定会带在身边。

However, as I wish for no war here, I wear soft clothes.

But if you are as bold as brave men affirm,

You will gladly grant me the good sport I demand

By right."

Then Arthur answer gave:

"If you, most noble knight,

Unarmoured combat crave,

We'll fail you not in fight."

13

"NO, it is not combat I crave, for come to that,

On this bench only beardless boys are sitting.

If I were hasped in armour on a high steed,

No man among you could match me, your might being meagre.

So I crave in this court a Christmas game,

For it is Yuletide and New Year, and young men abound here.

If any in this household is so hardy in spirit,

Of such mettlesome mind and so madly rash

As to strike a strong blow in return for another,

I shall offer to him this fine axe freely;

This axe, which is heavy enough, to handle as he please.

And I shall bide the first blow, as bare as I sit here.

If some intrepid man is tempted to try what I suggest,

我不想作战，因此穿了这身便装，
如果你们确实胆大而勇敢，
就爽快答应我公正的要求——
　　　好戏唱一场。"
　　亚瑟王听后声明：
　　"无比高尚的骑士，
　　如果你便装上阵，
　　我们不会伤害你。"

13

　　"不，我此行并不为作战，
因为在座诸位乳臭未干。
如果我全身披挂骑上战马，
你们力量不足，无人堪与厮杀。
我来这里只想玩玩圣诞游戏，
圣诞节和新年已来临，这儿有青年聚集，
此厅内是否有人意志坚强，
既精神饱满又疯狂而鲁莽，
我想把这斧子交给他，
让他先砍我一斧，然后由我偿还。
这斧足够沉重，用起来颇为顺手，
我赤手空拳坐在这里等待。
哪位勇士想上来一试身手，

Let him leap towards me and lay hold of this weapon,
Acquiring clear possession of it, no claim from me ensuing.
Then shall I stand up to his stroke, quite still on this floor—
So long as I shall have leave to launch a return blow
　　　Unchecked.
　　　Yet he shall have a year
　　　And a day's reprieve, I direct.
　　　Now hasten and let me hear
　　　Who answers, to what effect."

14

IF he had astonished them at the start, yet stiller now
Were the henchmen in hall, both high and low.
The rider wrenched himself round in his saddle
And rolled his red eyes about roughly and strangely,
Bending his brows, bristling and bright, on all,
His beard swaying as he strained to see who would rise.
When none came to accord with him, he coughed aloud,
Then pulled himself up proudly, and spoke as follows:
"What, is this Arthur's house, the honour of which
Is bruited abroad so abundantly?
Has your pride disappeared? Your prowess gone?
Your victories, your valour, your vaunts, where are they?

可以马上把这武器取走。

斧子一旦归他，我不会有二话，

那时我将一动不动站在地上，

唯一条件是允许我自由自在

　　　一斧砍还。

　　我还有话预先明示：

　　延期一年再加一天。

　　请大家不要再迟疑，

　　让我看看谁敢响应。"

14

似乎一开始大家已被他震慑，

在座的人无论尊卑都愈加沉默。

那骑士勒转马头，鞍上环视，

血红的眼睛转动着，显得粗野怪异，

两道眉毛紧锁，一根根竖立，

胡子飘拂着，想看看谁离座站起。

当发现无人响应，便故意大声咳嗽，

然后傲慢地勒住马，说出另一番话：

"怎么，这儿就是亚瑟的宫廷？

这样的地方据说也远扬声名？

难道你们的骄傲不存，英武已逝？

你们的胜利、豪气和自夸又在哪里？

The revel and renown of the Round Table

Is now overwhelmed by a word from one man's voice,

For all flinch for fear from a fight not begun!"

Upon this, he laughed so loudly that the lord grieved.

His fair features filled with blood

For shame.

He raged as roaring gale;

His followers felt the same.

The King, not one to quail,

To that cavalier then came.

15

"BY heaven," then said Arthur, "What you ask is foolish,

But as you firmly seek folly, find it you shall.

No good man here is aghast at your great words.

Hand me your axe now, for heaven's sake,

And I shall bestow the boon you bid us give."

He sprang towards him swiftly, seized it from his hand,

And fiercely the other fellow footed the floor.

Now Arthur had his axe, and holding it by the haft

Swung it about sternly, as if to strike with it.

The strong man stood before him, stretched to his full height,

Higher than any in the hall by a head and more.

如今仅仅因为我说了一句话，
圆桌的狂欢与声誉就已倒塌，
原来仗未开打，你们心里已害怕！"
说完，他哈哈大笑，弄得亚瑟十分难堪，
只见他由于羞愧变得

　　　面红耳赤，
　　亚瑟怒如咆哮的狂风，
　　他的骑士也火冒三丈，
　　这国王天生无所畏惧，
　　亲自来到那狂徒身旁。

15

"苍天在上，"亚瑟说，"你的要求很愚蠢，
既然你一意孤行，我可以遂你的愿。
你的大话吓不倒任何人，
看在老天的分上，请把斧子递给我，
你所要求的让我来履行。"
亚瑟一跃上前，从他手上取过斧子，
那骑士气势汹汹地站在地上，
亚瑟斧子在手，把斧柄握紧，
用力挥了挥，似乎就要往下劈。
大汉站在他面前，挺着身躯，
看上去比任何人都要高出一头有余。

Stern of face he stood there, stroking his beard,

Turning down his tunic in a tranquil manner,

Less umnmanned and dismayed by the mighty strokes

Than if a banqueter at the bench had brought him a drink

  Of wine.

   Then Gawain at Guinevere's side

   Bowed and spoke his design:

   "Before all, King, confide

   This fight to me. May it be mine."

16

"IF you would, worthy lord," said Gawain to the King,

"Bid me stir from this seat and stand beside you,

Allowing me without lese-majesty to leave the table,

And if my liege lady were not displeased thereby,

I should come there to counsel you before this court of nobles.

For it appears unmeet to me, as manners go,

When your hall hears uttered such a haughty request,

Though you gladly agree, for you to grant it yourself,

When on the benches about you many such bold men sit,

Under heaven, I hold, the highest-mettled,

There being no braver knights when battle is joined.

I am the weakest, the most wanting in wisdom, I know,

他神色凛然，一边还捻着胡子，
从容不迫地拉了拉外衣，
那坦然的神态根本不像要遭人斧砍，
倒像一位宾客坐在凳子上
　　品尝美酒。
　　高文坐在王后身边，
　　这时躬身请求国王：
　　"王上，这事交给我吧，
　　让我与他较量较量。"

16

　　"我的主人，"高文对国王说，
　　"如果允许我与您站在一起，
　　如果我要离座而不致失君臣之礼，
　　如果王后陛下没有什么异议，
　　我要当着大家的面劝阻您：
　　您的宫廷受到傲慢挑战，
　　尽管您自愿将责任承担，
　　但我总觉得这样做有违情理，
　　因为您周围坐着勇士一大帮，
　　我相信他们一个个顶天立地，
　　遇到战事，没有骑士比他们更勇敢。
　　我知道，我在他们中最弱最笨，

Any my life, if lost, would be least missed, truly.

Only through your being my uncle, am I to be valued;

No bounty but your blood in my body do I know.

And since this affair is too foolish to fall to you,

And I first asked it of you, make it over to me;

And if I fail to speak fittingly, let this full court judge

Without blame."

Then wisely they whispered of it,

And after, all said the same:

That the crowned King should be quit,

And Gawain given the game.

17

THEN the King commanded the courtly knight to rise.

He directly uprose, approached courteously,

Knelt low to his liege lord, laid hold of the weapon;

And he graciously let him have it, lifted up his hand

And gave him God's blessing, gladly urging him

To be strong in spirit and stout of sinew.

"Cousin, take care," said the King, "To chop once,

And if you strike with success, certainly I think

You will take the return blow without trouble in time.'

Gripping the great axe, Gawain goes to the man

如果我的性命丧失,损失也必然最轻。
只因您是我的舅父,我才被器重,
我身无长物,只是与您血脉相连,
今天的事落在您身上未免荒唐
因此我请求您让我接受挑战;
如果我说得不当,请诸位做出
　　善意评判。"
　　众骑士纷纷插话,
　　说到后来一致赞成:
　　国王位尊理应退下,
　　砍头游戏让与高文。

17

国王于是下令高贵的骑士站起身,
高文立即照办,彬彬有礼来到国王跟前;
他向国王鞠躬行礼,握住那件武器,
亚瑟郑重地把斧子交出,并将手举起,
给了他上帝的祝福和勉励,
愿他意志坚定、力量无穷。
"好外甥,你要小心,"国王吩咐,
"只许砍一斧,如果你砍他一举成功,
到时候他砍你也一定有吉无凶。"
高文提着大斧向那人走去,

Who awaits him unwavering, not quailing at all.

Then said to Sir Gawain the stout knight in green,

"Let us affirm our pact freshly, before going farther.

I beg you, bold sir, to be so good

As to tell me your true name, as I trust you to."

"In good faith," said the good knight, "Gawain is my name,

And whatever happens after, I offer you this blow,

And in twelve months' time I shall take the return blow

With whatever weapon you wish, and with no one else

      Shall I strive."

    The other with pledge replied,

    "I'm the merriest man alive

    It's a blow from you I must bide,

    Sir Gawain, so may I thrive."

18

"BY God," said the Green knight, "Sir Gawain, I rejoice

That I shall have from your hand what I have asked for here.

And you have gladly gone over, in good discourse,

The covenant I requested of the King in full,

Except that you shall assent, swearing in truth,

To seek me yourself, in such place as you think

To find me under the firmament, and fetch your payment

他一动不动等待着，毫无惧色。

强壮的绿衣骑士对高文说：

"动手之前，我们有话必须说在先，

我恳求你，勇敢的爵士，

请费心通报你的真实姓名。"

高尚的骑士说："请相信，高文是我名，

不管以后发生什么，我都要砍你这一斧，

十二个月过去，我会接受你的回砍，

那时不管你用什么武器，我一概不做

　　　任何反抗。"

　　那骑士发下誓言：

　　"我是世上最快活的人，

　　高文爵士，我等着你，

　　我的生命越砍越旺盛。"

18

"上帝做证，"骑士说，"高文爵士，

很高兴由你来把我的请求完成，

刚才我对国王所提的一切，

你都用得体的语言做了保证；

此外你还得对我发一个誓，

答应以后无论如何都要去找我，

到我所在的地方接受回报，

For what you deal me today before this dignified gathering."

"How shall I hunt for you? How find your home?"

Said Gawain, "By God that made me, I go in ignorance;

Nor, knight, do I konw your name or your court.

But instruct me truly thereof, and tell me your name,

And I shall wear out my wits to find my way there;

Here is my oath on it, in absolute honour!"

"That is enough this New Year, no more is needed,"

Said the gallant in green to Gawain the courteous,

"To tell you the truth, when I have taken the blow

After you have duly dealt it, I shall directly inform you

About my house and my home and my own name.

Then you may keep your covenant, and call on me,

And if I waft you no words, then well may you prosper,

Stay long in your own land and look for no further

   Trial.

  Now grip your weapon grim;

  Let us see your fighting style."

  "Gladly," said Gawain to him,

  Stroking the steel the while.

19

ON the ground the Green Knight graciously stood,

就为你今天所为，大家都将看见。"

高文说："让我如何找你？你的家何在？

创造我的主做证，我如今一无所知，

既不知你的姓名也不知你的宫廷，

请如实告诉我，说出你的名字，

我会想尽办法上那里去找你，

这是我的誓言，以我的名誉担保。"

"新年佳节无废话，你不必再说，"

绿衣骑士回答彬彬有礼的高文，

"实话对你说，我的家和姓名，

要等你把我砍，等你如愿以偿，

我才会说得直截了当。

那时你可以如约将我拜访；

如果我不能相告，你可以活得逍遥，

永远待在家乡，用不着再去

　　　　寻求试探。

　　现在请你捏紧大斧，

　　看看你武艺精不精。"

　　"那好哇，"高文一边说，

　　一边用手抚摸斧刃。

19

绿衣骑士恭恭敬敬站在地上，

With head slightly slanting to expose the flesh.

His long and lovely locks he laid over his crown,

Baring the naked neck for the business now due.

Gawain gripped his axe and gathered it on high,

Adavnced the left foot before him on the ground,

And slashed swiftly down on the exposed part,

So that the sharp blade sheared through, shattering the bones,

Sank deep in the sleek flesh, split it in two,

And the scintillating steel struck the ground.

The fair head fell from the neck, struck the floor,

And people spurned it as it rolled around.

Blood spurted from the body, bright against the green.

Yet the fellow did not fall, nor falter one whit,

But stoutly sprang forward on legs still sturdy,

Roughly reached out among the ranks of nobles,

Seized his splendid head and straightway lifted it.

Then he strode to his steed, snatched the bridle,

Stepped into the stirrup and swung aloft,

Holding his head in his hand by the hair.

He settled himself in the saddle as steadily

As if nothing had happened to him, though he had

      No head.

    He twisted his trunk about,

    That gruesome body that bled;

    He caused much dread and doubt

脑袋歪向一边,使皮肉露出

又长又美的头发甩到了脑后,

脖子裸露着,等待斧子砍下。

高文将他的武器高高举起,

左脚迈出一步向他靠近,

然后对准他裸露的部位飞快砍去,

锋利的斧刃一闪而过,骨头断裂,

斧子扎进厚厚的皮肉,脖颈一分为二,

闪亮的大斧这时已插在地上。

骑士的头从脖子上滚落,

当它滚过人们身边,大家用脚去踢[9],

鲜血从尸体中喷涌,绿莹莹一片。

然而,无头的家伙却连晃都没晃,

这时已跳起身,那脚步矫健依然。

他奋力在人群中挥动手臂,

抢过自己的头,将它高高举起。

然后奔向他的坐骑,抓住缰绳,

双脚套进马镫,在马背上摇动身躯,

那头被他抓住头发提在手里。

坐在马鞍上,他行动自如,

尽管头已断,这绿衣骑士却像

     无事一般。

   他扭动自己的腰板,

  无头躯体血流不止;

  当那断头张口开腔,

By the time his say was said.

FOR he held the head in his hand upright,

Pointed the face at the fairest in fame on the dais;

And it lifted its eyelids and looked glaringly,

And menacingly said with its mouth as you may now hear:

"Be prepared to perform what you promised, Gawain;

Seek faithfully till you find me, my fine fellow,

According to your oath in this hall in these knights' hearing.

Go to the Green Chapel without gainsaying to get

Such a stroke as you have struck. Strictly you deserve

That due redemption on the day of New Year.

As the Knight of the Green Chapel I am known to many;

Therefore if you ask for me, I shall be found.

So come, or else be called coward accordingly!"

Then he savagely swerved, sawing at the reins,

Rushed out at the hall door, his head in his hand,

And the flint-struck fire flew up from the hooves.

What place he departed to no person there knew,

Nor could any account be given of the country he had come from.

What then?

At the Green Knight Gawain and King

好不令人迷惑、心悸!

20

绿衣骑士用手举起自己的头,
把脸朝向回到座位上的著名骑士。
头上的眼睛张开了,射出凶狠的光,
那张嘴巴说出一番骇人的话:
"高文,准备去兑现自己的诺言吧,
我的好伙伴,请恪守当众许下的誓约,
老老实实去找我,直到找到为止。
不要食言,请去一所绿色教堂,
接受我的一斧,就像你砍了我那样,
就在新年那天,你会得到应有的回报。
许多人都知道,我是绿色教堂的骑士,
只要你向人打听,我们就能见面。
但如果不去,那你就成了懦夫!"
说完,绿衣骑士拉锯般急转身子,
手提着头,催马冲出宫廷大门,
马蹄击地如燧石取火,迸出一串串火星。
他后来去了哪里,无人知晓,
他生活的处所,在此无言奉告。

再说这边:
高文和国王拍手称快,

Grinned and laughed again;

But plainly approved the thing

As a marvel in the world of men.

21

THOUGH honoured King Arthur was at heart astounded,

He let no sign of it be seen, but said clearly

To the comely queen in courtly speech,

"Do not be dismayed, dear lay, today:

Such cleverness comes well at Christmastide,

Like the playing of interludes, laughter and song,

As lords and ladies delight in courtly carols.

However, I am now able to eat the repast,

Having seen, I must say, a sight to wonder at."

He glanced at Sir Gawain, and gracefully said,

"Now sir, hang up your axe: you have hewn enough."

And on the backcloth above the dais it was boldly hung

Where all men might mark it and marvel at it

And with truthful testimony tell the wonder of it.

Then to the table the two went together,

The King and the constant knight, and keen men served them

Double portions of each dainty with all due dignity,

All manner of meat, and minstrelsy too.

绿衣骑士成了笑柄，

但他们也坦言不讳，

此类怪事闻所未闻。

21

尽管尊敬的国王内心惊异非常，

但没有让人觉察他有些慌张，

他彬彬有礼地对高贵的王后说：

"亲爱的夫人，请你别沮丧，

这场游戏正好给圣诞节助兴，

就像善男信女欢唱圣诞颂歌，

歌声中应该伴和着笑声。

我得说，奇迹已亲眼所见，

现在可以安心地享用酒宴。"

他看了一眼高文，又接着说，

"爵士，你砍够了，把斧子挂起吧。"

斧子于是被高挂在厅堂后的幕帐上，

人人能看见，人人能为之惊叹，

作为奇迹的见证将它的故事传扬。

国王和忠诚的骑士回到座位，

机敏的仆役为他们端上加倍的佳肴，

恭敬地添上各式各样的肉食。

吟游诗人则唱起古老的歌。

Daylong they delighted till darkness came
To their shores.
Now Gawain give a thought,
Lest peril make you pause
In seeking out the sport
That you have claimed as yours.

就这样，他们整天举杯畅饮，直到黑夜

降临海岸。

高文此时暗下决心，

尽管前途吉凶未知，

但他不会畏惧不前，

把自己的誓约背弃。

FIT II

22

SUCH earnest of noble action had Arthur at New Year,

For he was avid to hear exploits vaunted.

Though starved of such speeches when seated at first,

Now had they high matter indeed, their hands full of it.

Gawain was glad to begin the games in hall,

But though the end be heavy, have no wonder,

For if men are spritely in spirit after strong drink,

Soon the year slides past, never the same twice;

There is no foretelling its fulfilment from the start.

Yes, this Yuletide passed and the year following;

Season after season in succession went by.

After Christmas comes the crabbed Lenten time,

Which forces on the flesh fish and food yet plainer.

Then weather more vernal wars with the wintry world,

The cold ebbs and declines, the clouds lift,

In shining showers the rain sheds warmth

第二章

22

每逢新年伊始，亚瑟便向往建功立业，
渴望听到人们将他的功勋颂扬。
原先只期望大家坐下来叙谈一番，
谁想真正的冒险被他们碰上。
尽管前途险恶，这一点不用怀疑，
高文却乐意由他开演这场游戏。
男人们喝多了酒精神亢奋，
不知不觉节日已过，一去不返；
岁月如何流逝谁也不能预言。
不错，圣诞节已结束，新的一年开始，
季节一个连着一个，不断交替，
圣诞过后便是难熬的封斋期，
这期间人们只能戒荤食素。
接着春天的气息逐渐将严冬战胜，
寒流向后退却、衰微，白云升上蓝天，
晶莹的阵雨伴随着温煦的春光，

And falls upon the fair plain, where flowers appear;
The grassy lawns and groves alike are garbed in green;
Birds prepare to build, and brightly sing
The solace of the ensuing summer that soothes hill

And dell.
By hedgerows rank and rich
The blossoms bloom and swell,
And sounds of sweetest pitch
From lovely woodlands well.

23

THEN comes the season of summer with soft winds,
When Zephyrus himself breathes on seeds and herbs.
In paradise is the plant that springs in the open
When the dripping dew drops from its leaves,
And it bears the blissful gleam of the bright sun.
Then Harvest comes hurrying, urging it on,
Warning it because of winter to wax ripe soon;
He drives the dust to rise with the drought he brings,
Forcing it to fly up from the face of the earth.
Wrathful winds in raging skies wrestle with the sun;
Leaves are lashed loose from the trees and lie on the ground
And the grass becomes grey which was green before.

52

降落在美丽的平川,使鲜花开放;
鸟儿开始筑巢,为即将来临的盛夏,
欢快地歌唱,山冈谷地的美景,

　　　令它们神往。
　　繁茂的灌木丛边,
　　花儿正开得欢畅,
　　优美无比的乐音,
　　在树林子里飘荡。

23

当仄费洛斯[10]呵气给种子和野草,
夏季随着柔和的风降临。
野外勃发的草木享受天堂般的欢乐,
露珠子不断地从叶梢滴落,
灿烂的阳光映照其上,闪闪发光。
随后收获的季节匆匆而至,
催促果实快快成熟,因为冬季就在前头。
大地由于干燥腾起尘埃,
飞飞扬扬地弥漫在空中。
暴怒的狂风在天际与太阳角斗;
树叶被它从树梢打落地上,
绿油油的草地成了一片灰黄,

What rose from root at first now ripens and rots;

So the year in passing yields its many yesterdays,

And winter returns, as the way of the world is,

   I swear;

   So came the Michaelmas moon,

   With winter threatening there,

   And Gawain considered soon

   The fell way he must fare.

24

YET he stayed in hall with Arthur till All Saints' Day,

When Arthur provided plentifully, especially for Gawain,

A rich feast and high revelry at the Round Table.

The gallant lords and gay ladies grieved for Gawain,

Anxious on his account; but all the same

They mentioned only matters of mirthful import,

Joylessly joking for that gentle knight's sake.

For after dinner with dropping heart he addreesed his uncle

And spoke plainly of his departure, putting it thus:

"Now, liege lord of my life, I beg my leave of you.

You know the kind of covenant it is: I care little

To tell over the trais of it, trifling as they are,

But I am bound to bear the blow and must be gone tomorrow

从根部萌芽的植物成熟了,腐败了,

岁月在流逝中养育无数个昨日,

冬回大地,自然的法则就是如此,

　　　我敢打赌;

　　转眼到了米迦勒节

　　严冬正一天天逼近,

　　高文猛然想起誓约:

　　他得冒险外出旅行。

24

他在亚瑟的宫廷一直待到万圣节,

这一天,亚瑟在圆桌设宴,

特意备下丰盛的酒席为他饯行。

勇敢的勋爵和快活的女士都为他伤心,

为他焦虑;大伙儿心照不宣,

只讲一些愉快的事给他听,

但因为这位善良的骑士,谁也笑不起来。

宴席后高文怀着沉重的心情

向他的舅父辞别,他这样说:

"国王陛下,我的主人,我这就向您告辞,

您知道这是何样的一个誓约,

我无心谈论它,尽管这考验无足轻重,

但我一定得承领那一斧,凭借上帝指引,

To seek the gallant in green, as God sees fit to guide me."

Then the most courtly in that company came together,

Ywain and Eric and others in troops,

Sir Dodinal the Fierce, The Duke of Clarence,

Lancelot and Lionel and Lucan the Good,

Sir Bors and Sir Bedivere, both strong men,

And many admired knights, with Mador of the Gate.

All the company of the court came near to the King

With carking care in their hearts, to counsel the knight.

Much searing sorrow was suffered in the hall

That such a gallant man as Gawain should go in quest

To suffer a savage blow, and his sword no more

      Should bear.

    Said Gawain, gay of cheer,

    "Whether fate be foul or fair,

    Why falter I or fear?

    What should man do but dare?"

25

HE dwelt there all that day, and at dawn on the morrow

Asked for his armour. Every item was brought.

First a crimson carpet was cast over the floor

And the great pile of gilded war-gear glittered upon it.

明天就登程寻找绿衣骑士。"

这时,高贵的骑士一个个走过来,

他们中有雨文和埃里克,

勇猛的道德纳尔,他是克拉伦斯的公爵,

朗斯洛、莱纳尔和好人儿卢卡恩,

鲍斯和比德维,他两人武艺超群,

此外还有许多著名骑士,包括盖特的梅达。

这一大班豪杰来到国王跟前,

怀着关切的心情为高文出谋划策。

悲哀笼罩整座宴会厅,

人人为壮士高文的命运担忧,

因为他得赤手空拳去寻求——

　　　　野蛮的一斧。

　　乐呵呵的高文说:

　　"命运吉凶无所谓,

　　我何必提心吊胆?

　　男子汉何事难为?"

25

这天他在王宫下榻,次日凌晨,

他让人取来盔甲和其他装备。

深红的地毯铺在地板上,

镀金的战服和兵器闪闪发光。

The strong man stepped on it, took the steel in hand.

The doublet he dressed in was dear Turkestan stuff;

Then came the courtly cape, cut with skill,

Finely lined with fur, and fastened close.

Then they set the steel shoes on the strong man's feet,

Lapped his legs in steel with lovely greaves,

Complete with knee-pieces, polished bright

And connecting at the knee with gold-knobbed hinges.

Then came the cuisses, which cunningly enclosed

His thighs thick of thew, and which thongs secured.

Next the hauberk, interlinked with argent steel rings

Which rested on rich material, wrapped the warrior round.

He had polished armour on arms and elbows,

Glinting and gay, and gloves of metal,

And all the goodly gear to give help whatever

     Betide;

   With surcoat richly wrought,

   Gold spurs attached in pride,

   A silken sword-belt athwart,

   And steadfast blade at his side.

26

WHEN he was hasped in armour his harness was noble;

壮士走上去,将宝剑拿在手里。
他穿的紧身衣是突厥斯坦的织品;
华美的披肩缝制得极其精巧,
边上饰有一圈皮毛,将肩膀紧紧护住。
众人帮壮士穿上战靴,
用漂亮的胫甲套住他的小腿。
那一整套金灿的护膝甲,
由金制的圆头铰链与胫甲连接,
他那肌肉结实的大腿也围有护甲,
狭长的皮带将它牢牢扎住。
再上方是用银环扣住的锁子铠,
银环套在甲片间,围了武士一身。
手臂和肘部,也有闪亮的甲片保护,
就连他的手套,也由金属制成。
不管碰到什么事,这身武装足以让他
　　　　有备无患;
　　　铠外长氅华美无比,
　　　金制马刺气派非凡,
　　　丝绸腰带拦腰横系,
　　　纯钢宝剑挂在一旁。

26

他全副武装,高贵非凡,

The least lace or loop was lustrous with gold.

So, harnessed as he was, he heard his mass

As it was offered at the high altar in worship.

Then he came to the King and his court-fellows,

Took leave with loving courtesy of lord and lady,

Who commended him to Christ and kissed him farewell.

By now Gringolet had been got ready, and girt with a saddle

That gleamed most gaily with many golden fringes,

Everywhere nailed newly for this noble occasion.

The bridle was embossed and bound with bright gold;

So were the furnishings of the fore-harness and the fine skirts.

The crupper and the caparison accorded with the saddle-bows,

And all was arrayed on red with nails of richest gold,

Which glittered and glanced like gleams of the sun.

Then his casque, equipped with clasps of great strength

And padded inside, he seized and swiftly kissed;

It towered high on his head and was hasped at the back,

With a brilliant silk band over the burnished neck-guard,

Embroidered and bossed with the best gems

On broad silken borders, with birds about the seams,

Such as parrots painted with periwinkles between,

And turtles and true-love-knots traced as thickly

As if many beauties in a bower had been busy seven winters

        Thereabout.

    The circlet on his head

浑身上下无处不闪耀着金光。

等一切拾掇停当,他就去听弥撒,

就像往日在神坛前所做的那样。

然后他来到国王和同僚那里,

彬彬有礼地向他们辞行;

大家在基督前赞美他,与他吻别。

这时,格林哥莱[11]也已经备好鞍辔,

无数串金色的流苏在它身上闪耀,

为了这次神圣的旅行,新换了整套马具。

金色的嚼子雕有各种图案;

马鞍的前部和鞍褥金光闪闪。

尾鞯和马服则与前穿颜色一致,

连接处排满了金制的扣子,

闪闪耀耀犹如照射的阳光。

全副武装的高文见马踏步进来,

一把将它抓住,热烈地亲吻它;

那马在他身边显得异常高大,

护颈甲上还围了一根宽宽的缎带,

饰边镶嵌着最珍贵的宝石,

缎面绣有许多小鸟的图案,

鹦鹉、斑鸠在长春花丛中栖息,

此外还有密密麻麻的同心结[12],

也许无数闺秀为此忙碌过整整

　　　　七个冬天。

　　高文的头上还有饰环,

Was prized more precious no doubt,

And perfectly diamonded,

Threw a gleaming lustre out.

27

THEN they showed him the shield of shining gules,

With the Pentangle in pure gold depicted thereon.

He brandished it by the baldric, and about his neck

He slung it in a seemly way, and it suited him well.

And I intend to tell you, though I tarry therefore,

Why the Pentangle is proper to this prince of knights.

It is a symbol which Solomon conceived once

To betoken holy truth, by its intrinsic right,

For it is a figure which has five points,

And each line overlaps and is locked with another;

And it is endless everywhere, and the English call it,

In all the land, I hear, the Endless Knot.

Therefore it goes with Sir Gawain and his gleaming armour,

For, ever faithful in five things, each in fivefold manner,

Gawain was reputed good and, like gold well refined,

He was devoid of all villainy, every virtue displaying

      In the field.

      Thus this Pentangle new

那价值更加不菲，

里面镶嵌着钻石，

放射出熠熠光辉。

27

然后大伙给他拿来一面红盾，

上面绘有一颗镀金的五角星。

高文手持佩带将盾一挥，把它挂上脖颈，

看得出这盾他很合手。

尽管我不愿离题，但我还是要告诉你，

为何五角星该由这骑士王子佩戴。

五角星是所罗门设计的标识，

内部结构合理，用来表示神圣真理，

因为它有五个尖端，

每条线都交叉，连锁在一起；

没有断点，在我们英国各地，

我听说人们都管它叫"不断的结"。

高文与它同在，并将它标上盔甲，

因为他具备五种美德、五重操行，

他因此享有美誉，如金子般纯洁，

一切丑恶与他无涉，而每种美德却

　　　　处处体现。

　　这颗崭新的五角星，

He carried on coat and shield,
As a man of troth most true
And knightly name annealed.

28

FIRST he was found faultless in his five wits.

Next, his five fingers never failed the knight,

And all his trust on earth was in the five wounds

Which came to Christ on the Cross, as the Creed tells.

And whenever the bold man was busy on the battlefield,

Through all other things he thought on this,

That his prowess all depended on the five pure Joys

That the holy Queen of Heaven had of her Child.

Accordingly the courteous knight had that queen's image

Etched on the inside of his armoured shield,

So that when he beheld her, his heart did not fail.

The fifth five I find the famous man practised

Were—Liberality and Lovingkindness leading the rest;

Then his Continence and Courtesy, which were never corrupted;

And Piety, the surpassing virtue. These pure five

Were more firmly fixed on that fine man

Than on any other, and every multiple,

Each interlocking with another, had no end,

就这样标识在盾上，
只因他是个实诚人，
骑士的美名不虚妄。

28

首先，他具有无疵无瑕的五智[13]，
其次，他有不辱骑士荣名的五指，
他在人间的信仰是那五个伤口，
经书说，五伤来自十字架上的基督。
每当这位勇士征战在沙场，
脑子里总是这样思量：
他的勇力全仰仗五大欢喜[14]，
这欢喜圣母临产时就曾经历。
因此，这位彬彬有礼的骑士
便将圣母像刻在盾的背面，
只要看见它，他就不会丧失信心。
我发现这"五"还有第五种含义，
即慷慨、仁慈、克制、谦恭和虔诚。
这位著名人物身体力行，
非凡的美德从未受玷污。
这一切都牢牢在他身上扎根，
没有人能与他相提并论，
在这里每个"五"都相互叠加，相互交错，

Being fixed to five points which never failed,

Never assembling on one side, nor sundering either,

With no end at any angle; nor can I find

Where the design started or procceded to its end.

Thus on his shining shield this knot was shaped

Royally in red gold upon red gules.

That is the pure Pentangle, so people who are wise

    Are taught.

      Now Gawain was ready and gay;

      His spear he promptly caught

      And gave them all good day

      For ever, as he thought.

29

HE struck the steed with his spurs and sprang on his way

So forcefully that the fire flew up from the flinty stones.

All who saw that seemly sight were sick at heart,

And all said to each other softly, in the same breath,

In care for that comely knight, "By Christ, it is evil

That yon lord should be lost, who lives so nobly!

To find his fellow on earth in faith is not easy.

It would have been wiser to have worked more warily,

And to have dubbed the dear man a duke of the realm.

连续不断,固定在五个循环的点上,
没有哪一方偏重,哪一方断裂,
任何一个锐角都不是它的终极;
我看不出这个图案有何缺陷。
不断的结就这样标上明亮的盾,
气派非凡,红色表面上金光耀眼!
这就是纯洁的五角星,贤明者
　　　　都曾听说。

　　快活的高文备好行装,
　　敏捷地接过一支长矛,
　　然后——惜别众伙伴,
　　从内心祝愿他们安好。

29

他用踢马刺催赶骏马上路,
马蹄猛击地面,坚硬的石头冒出火星。
见此情景人人心里都难受,
大伙私语,都对骑士表示关切:
"基督做证,这爵爷一生高尚,
如此忠义之士世间屈指可数,
此番如一去不回,该多么令人遗憾!
当初这事本该处理得更谨慎,
这个可亲的人应该被敕封公爵。

A magnificent master of men he might have been,

And so had a happier fate than to be utterly destroyed,

Beheaded by an unearthly being out of arrogance.

Who supposed the Prince would approve such counsel

As is giddily given in Christmas games by knights?"

Many were the watery tears that whelmed from weeping eyes,

When on quest that worthy knight went from the court

      That day.

    He faltered not nor feared,

    But quickly went his way;

    His road was rough and weird,

    Or so the stories say.

30

NOW the gallant Sir Gawain in God's name goes

Riding through the realm of Britain, no rapture in his mind.

Often the long night he lay alone and companionless,

And did not find in front of him food of his choice;

He had no comrade tbut his courser in the country woods and hills,

No traveller to talk to on the track but God,

Till he was nearly nigh to Northern Wales.

The isles of Anglesey he kept always on his left,

And fared across the fords by the foreshore

他可以成为伟大的公国君主，
应该有更好的命运，
而不该被野蛮人砍头毁去前程。
圣诞游戏时的许诺本来就随便，
谁想他竟把它看得那么认真!"
那天,眼巴巴看着骑士出宫探险,
许多人眼里早已是——
　　　　泪水涟涟。
　　他没有心悸胆寒,
　　一路上快马加鞭,
　　他前路坎坷艰难,
　　诚如说书者所言。

30

勇敢的高文爵士任上帝指引,
闷闷不乐,骑马穿越不列颠。
漫长的黑夜他常常独自度过,
享用什么食物更无法由自己挑选;
荒山野岭中,只有骏马与他为伴,
一路上除了上帝没有人可以交谈,
就这样,他来到了北部威尔士附近。
他一直沿安格尔西岛往左走,
趁海水退潮时渡过浅水滩,

Over at Holy Head to the other side

Into the wilderness of Wirral, where few dwelled

To whom God or good-hearted man gave his love.

And always as he went, he asked whomever he met

If they knew or had knowledge of a knight in green,

Or could guide him to the ground where a green chapel stood.

And there was none but said him nay, for never in their lives

Had they set eyes on someone of such a hue

      As green.

   His way was wild and strange

   By dreary hill and dean.

   His mood would many times change

   Before that fane was seen.

31

HE rode far from his friends, a forsaken man,

Scaling many cliffs in country unknown.

At every bank or beach where the brave man crossed water,

He found a foe in front of him, except by a freak of chance,

And so foul and fierce a one that he was forced to fight.

So many marvels did the man meet in the mountains,

It would be too tedious to tell a tenth of them.

He had death-struggles with dragons, did battle with wolves,

再经霍利黑德到达岛的另一边，

然后进入蛮荒的威勒尔，[15]那里人烟罕见，

上帝和善心人的仁爱无从施行。

一路上不管碰见谁，他便上前询问

他们是否知道有位绿衣骑士，

能否给他指出通向一所绿色教堂的道路。

然而，没有人能给他肯定的回答，

都说一生中从没见过此等——

    绿衣怪人。

  他的道路蜿蜒在深山，

  那里既荒凉又陌生。

  他的心绪混乱如麻，

  除非见到那所教堂。

31

他背井离乡，远离自己的伙伴，

在无名的荒野攀登无数的岩壁。

勇士每跨越一道河堤、一片浅滩，

除非福星高照，免不了与强敌相遇，

对手来势汹汹，他不得已只好应战。

在深山老林，他经历过许多怪事，

在此哪怕只说十分之一，也未免乏味冗长。

他还曾与巨龙殊死鏖战，与恶狼搏斗，

Warred with wild men who dwelt among the crags,

Battled with bulls and bears and boars at other times,

And ogres that panted after him on the high fells.

Had he not been doughty in endurance and dutiful to God,

Doubtless he would have been done to death time and again.

Yet the warring little worried him; worse was the winter,

When the cold clear water cascaded from the clouds

And froze before it could fall to the fallow earth.

Half-slain by the sleet, he slept in his armour

Night after night among the naked rocks,

Where the cold streams splashed from the steep crests

Or hung high over his head in hard icicles.

So in peril and pain, in parlous plight,

This knight covered the country till Christmas Eve

  Alone;

  And he that eventide

  To Mary made his moan,

  And begged her be his guide

  Till some shelter should be shown.

32

MERRILY in the morning by a mountain he rode

Into a wondrously wild wooded cleft,

与居住山洞的野人交手，

有时还与野牛、熊和野猪交锋，

在荒山野岭，还有魔怪在背后紧紧追赶。

如果他不够勇敢，不恭顺上帝，

无疑已经死过无数次。

但他并不在意厮杀，更糟的是那天气，

清冷的雨水从云层倾泻，

尚未落到荒地上，已经结成冰霜。

许多个夜晚，他躺在光滑的岩石丛中，

裹着盔甲而睡，身体被冰雹冻僵，

更何况寒冷的溪水在周身飞溅，

有时坚硬冰锥就悬在他的头顶！

就这样，这位骑士历经艰难困苦，

为履行诺言，走遍天南地北，直到

　　　　圣诞前夕。

　　　就在那天的黄昏，

　　　他向玛丽亚诉苦，

　　　请求她指点迷津，

　　　让他有客店投宿。

32

那天上午，他骑马悠然地沿山脚行走，

最后进入一道周遭长满树木的奇妙山口，

With high hills on each side overpeering a forest

Of huge hoary oaks, a hundred together.

The hazel and the hawthorn were intertwined

With rough ragged moss trailing everywhere,

And on the bleak branches birds in misery

Piteously piped away, pinched with cold.

The gallant knight on Gringolet galloped under them

Through many a swamp and marsh, a man all alone,

Fearing lest he should fail, through adverse fortune,

To see the service of him who that same night

Was born of a bright maiden to banish our strife.

And so sighing he said, "I beseech thee Lord,

And thee Mary, mildest mother so dear,

That in some haven with due honour I may hear Mass

And Matins tomorrow morning: meekly I ask it,

And promptly thereto I pray my Pater and Ave

   And Creed."

  He crossed himself and cried

  For his sins, and said, "Christ speed

  My cause, his cross my guide!"

  So prayed he, spurring his steed.

两旁陡峭的高山俯视下面山涧，

那里有一片橡树林，百来棵光景。

榛木和山楂树杂生其间，

破衣烂裳般的苔藓随处可见。

阴冷的树枝上，鸟儿冻得缩着身子，

凄惨地尖声鸣叫，令人陡生怜悯！

骑士驱使格林哥莱在林间疾驰，

孤身一人穿过一片片沼泽地，

他担心厄运作弄他，使他无缘望弥撒，

那仪式为纪念该日出生的一个人，

他从处女降生，为的是平息人间纷争。

骑士叹息说："主啊，我祈求你，

祈求最最慈祥的圣母玛丽亚，

让我有幸在什么地方听听弥撒，

并参加明天的晨祷；我在此恭顺地请求，

让我有缘听到主祷文、颂歌，以及

　　　　教规的颂扬。"

　　他画十字向主请罪：

　　"建功立业全凭基督，

　　十字架请指引我！"

　　说完催马继续赶路。

33

THRICE the sign of the Saviour on himself he had made,

When in the wood he was aware of a dwelling with a moat

On a promontory above a plateau, penned in by the boughs

And tremendous trunks of trees, and trenched about;

The comeliest castle that ever a knight owned,

It was pitched on a plain, with a park all round,

Impregnably palisaded with pointed stakes,

And containing many trees in its two-mile circumference.

The courteous knight contemplated the castle from one side

As it shimmered and shone through the shining oaks.

Then humbly he took off his helmet and offered thanks

To Jesus and Saint Julian, gentle patrons both,

Who had given him grace and gratified his wish.

"Now grant it be good lodging!" the gallant knight said.

Then he goaded Gringolet with his golden heels,

And mostly by chance emerged on the main highway,

Which brought the brave man to the bridge's end

        With one cast.

     The drawbridge vertical,

     The gates shut firm and fast,

     The well-provided wall—

33

高文终于在林间发现一个处所，

不禁喜出望外，在胸前连画三个十字，

那座建筑坐落在一个岬角上，

一条壕沟环护着，参天大树将它遮蔽；

它是骑士所拥有的最好城堡，

屹立在山野，周围就是花园，

尖头的栅柱将它围护得无懈可击，

方园二英里内尽是高大树木。

谦逊的骑士从一边观察，

只见城堡在橡树林背后熠熠生辉。

他摘下头盔，向两位仁慈的恩主——

基督和圣朱利安[16]致以诚挚的谢意，

他们施予他恩惠，使他心满意足。

"这一定是个好处所！"勇敢的骑士说。

他用金色的马刺将格林哥莱驱赶，

不知不觉来到一条大道上，

沿着这条道路一直来到

       吊桥跟前。

    那吊桥高高悬垂，

    那城门紧紧关闭，

    护城墙坚不可摧，

It blenched at never a blast.

34

THE knight, still on his steed, stayed on the bank

Of the deep double ditch that drove round the place.

The wall went into the water wonderfully deep,

And then to a huge height upwards it reared

In hard hewn stone, up to the cornice;

Built under the battlements in the best style, courses jutted

And turrets protruded between, constructed

With loopholes in plenty with locking shutters.

No better barbican had ever been beheld by that knight.

And inside he could see a splendid high hall

With towers and turrets on top, all tipped with crenellations,

And pretty pinnacles placed along its length,

With carved copes, cunningly worked.

Many chalk-white chimneys the chevalier saw

On the tops of towers twinkling whitely,

So many painted pinnacles sprinkled everywhere,

Congregated in clusters among the crenellations,

That it appeared like a prospect of paper patterning.

To the gallant knight on Gringolet it seemed good enough

If he could ever gain entrance to the inner court,

风雨中傲然屹立。

34

骑士骑马立在壕沟的堤岸上，
那深深的壕沟环绕城堡一周。
护城墙用经过劈削的坚石砌成，
墙基筑在深不可测的水里，
它高高耸立着，一直达到屋檐。
漂亮的屋脊层层叠叠从雉堞上冒出，
角楼屹立其间，上面每个孔眼
都装有一道森严的遮门。
这样的外堡高文平生还是初次看见。
再往内看，还有一座雄伟的厅堂，
高处有塔楼和角楼，射箭孔鳞次栉比，
漂亮的尖阁有序地出现在屋脊处，
墙帽经过雕饰，那工艺无比精巧。
骑士还注意到许多白色的烟囱，
在塔楼上闪耀着银色的光芒，
经过装饰的尖阁林立在射箭孔上方，
看上去一串串不知凡几，
那景象好像一幅纸剪的图案。[17]
格林哥莱身上的骑士思忖：
在此人人欢庆的圣诞佳节，

And harbour in that house while Holy Day lasted,

    We cheered.

    He hailed, and at a height

    A civil porter appeared,

    Who welcomed the wandering knight,

    And his inquiry heard.

35

"GOOD sir," said Gawain, "Will you give my message

To the high lord of this house, that I ask for lodging?"

"Yes, by Saint Peter," replied the porter, "and I think

You may lodge here as long as you like, sir knight."

Then away he went eagerly, and swiftly returned

With a host of well-wishers to welcome the knight.

They let down the drawbridge and in a dignified way

Came out and did honour to him, kneeling

Courteously on the cold ground to accord him worthy welcome.

They prayed him to pass the portcullis, now pulled up high,

And he readily bid them rise and rode over the bridge.

Servants held his saddle while he stepped down,

And his steed was stabled by sturdy men in plenty.

Strong knights and squires descended then

To bring the bold warrier blithely into hall.

他如果能进入城堡歇足,那真是——

天大的乐事。

他于是向里打招呼,

一位哨兵来到城头,

他欢迎漫游的骑士,

乐意听他说明来由。

35

"好伙计,"高文说,"能否帮我传个话,

告诉城堡的主人,就说我想在贵府借宿?"

"圣彼得做证,"哨兵说,"骑士老爷,

这没问题,你愿意住多久都可以。"

说完他连忙下去,一会儿以后,

随一位管事返回,迎接来访的骑士。

他们将吊桥放下,恭敬地走出城门,

为表示欢迎的诚意,还在寒冷的地上

礼数周全地行了屈膝大礼。

他们请他进入高高升起的闸门,

他赶紧请他们站起,然后骑马通过吊桥。

下马时仆役们为他扶住马鞍,

那骏马被一班壮汉牵进了马房。

然后过来几位骑士和绅士,

欣喜地迎接勇敢的战士进入大厅,

When he took off his helmet, many hurried forward

To receive it and so serve this stately man,

And his bright sword and buckler were both taken as well.

Then graciously he greeted each gallant knight,

And many proud men pressed forward to pay their respects.

Garbed in his fine garments, he was guided to the hall,

Where a fine fire was burning fiercely on the hearth.

Then the prince of those people appeared from his chamber

To meet in mannerly style the man in his hall.

"You are welcome to dwell here as you wish," he said,

'Treat everything as your own, and have what you please

       In this place."

    "I yield my best thank yet:

    May Christ make good your grace!"

    Said Gawain and, gladly met,

    They clasped in close embrace.

36

GAWAIN gazed at the gallant who had greeted him well

And it seemed to him the stronghold possessed a brave lord,

A powerful man in his prime, of stupendous size,

Broad and bright was his beard, all beaver-hued;

Strong and sturdy he stood on his stalwart legs;

当他摘下头盔,便有一班人急忙上前,
将头盔接去,忙不迭地向他献殷勤。
他于是将闪亮的剑和盾也一道卸下,
优雅大方地与众骑士寒暄;
他们则蜂拥上前向他表示敬意。
戎装的高文被大家带到厅堂,
那里有一壁炉火烧得正旺。
城堡主这时从自己的房里出来,
很有礼貌地接见高文。
"欢迎你来此歇足,"他说,
"请不要见外,这里的一切都
　　　　任阁下差遣。"
　　"我衷心地向你致谢,
　　愿主佑你福星高照。"
　　高文高兴地迎过去,
　　与主人热烈地拥抱。

36

高文仔细打量这位盛情接待他的人,
在他眼里,此人犹如一座堡垒,
具有强大的力量、伟岸的身躯,
蓄着一把大胡子,颜色如河狸;
两条粗壮的大腿显得格外强劲有力;

His face was fierce as fire, free was his speech,

And he seemed in good sooth a suitable man

To be prince of a people with companions of mettle.

This prince led him to an apartment and expressly commanded

That a man be commissioned to minister to Gawain;

And at his bidding a band of men bent to serve

Brought him to a beautiful room where the bedding was noble.

The bed-curtains, of brilliant silk with bright gold hems,

Had skilfully-sewn coverlets with comely facings,

And the fairest fur on the fringes was worked.

With ruddy gold rings on the cords ran the curtains;

Toulouse and Turkestan tapestries on the wall

And fine capets underfoot, on the floor, were fittingly matched.

There amid merry talk the man was disrobed,

And stripped of his battle-sark and his splendid clothes.

Retainers readily brought him rich robes

Of the choicest knid to choose from and change into.

In a trice when he took one, and was attired in it,

And it sat on him in style, with spreading skirts,

It certainly seemed to those assembled as if spring

In all its hues were evident before them;

His lithe limbs below the garment were gleaming with beauty.

Jesus never made, so men judged, more gentle and handsome

       A knight:

  From wherever in the world he were,

脸上横眉竖眼,像燃着一团火,
谈吐无所顾忌,说句大实话,
他似乎天生就是豪强中的霸主。
主人领高文进入寓所,
明确指令要有专人伺候;
在主人的吩咐下,许多人甘愿为他服务,
他们把他带进一间豪华的卧室。
那丝绸床帷有着金光闪闪的折边,
床罩做工精细,饰面美观适宜,
边缘处还饰有优质毛皮,
垂挂床帷的带子装饰金制套环,
墙上挂着图卢兹和突厥斯坦的织锦,
地上铺有地毯,色彩鲜艳、搭配和谐。
在快乐的谈笑声中,高文卸下盔甲,
脱去那套光彩夺目的骑士武装;
仆役们赶紧为他拿来华丽的长袍,
那服装是上等的织物,稀世珍品。
他接过其中一件,很快穿上身,
那长袍有宽大的下摆,很适合他的身段。
聚集在场的人见了他这副装扮,
都以为是五彩缤纷的春天来到身旁。
长袍下他的肢体显得异常柔美,
大家都说,基督创造的骑士数他
　　　最高雅英俊。
　　不管他来自世界何方,

At sight it seemed he might
Be a prince without a peer
In field where fell men fight.

37

AT the chimmeyed hearth where charcoal burned, a chair was placed
For Sir Gawain in gracious style, gorgeously decked
With cushions on quilted work, both cunningly wrought;
And then on that man a magnificent mantle was thrown,
A gleaming garment gorgeously embroidered,
Fairly lined with fur, the finest skins
Of ermine on earth, and his hood of the same.
In that splendid seat he sat in dignity,
And warmth came to him at once, bringing well-being.
In a trice on fine trestles a table was put up,
Then covered with a cloth shining clean and white,
And set with silver spoons, salt-cellars and overlays.
The worthy knight washed willingly, and went to his meat.
In seemly enough style servants brought him
Several fine soups, seasoned lavishly
Twice-fold, as is fitting, and fish of all kinds—
Some baked in bread, some browned on coals,
Some seethed, some stewed and savoured with spice,

看见他的人无不认为，

在那群雄纷争的战场，

他足称王子无人比匹。

37

直通屋顶的炉膛燃烧着炭火，

仆役们为高文摆了张舒适的椅子，

华丽的坐垫是件做工精巧的刺绣品；

他们在他身上又添了件华丽披风，

这披风绣得金光耀眼，

衬里镶皮毛，用的是最好的貂皮，

连那兜帽也是貂皮制品。

他就这样雍容华贵地坐在椅子上，

暖意传遍周身，使他爽快非常。

不一会，屋子里摆下一张桌子，

上面盖了干净洁白的餐布，

银匙和盐罐等也一一摆放整齐。

高贵的骑士洗过脸，接着便开始就餐。

仆人们为他端上几盘羹汤，

那汤调料丰富，鲜美异常，

此外还有各种各样的鱼——

有夹面包中焙的，有经炭火烤的，

还有煮的、炖的、加过香料的，

But always subtly sauced, and so the man liked it.

The gentle knight generously judged it a feast,

And often said so, while the servers spurred hm on thus

As he ate:

"This present penance do;

It soon shall be offset."

The knight rejoiced anew,

For the wine his spirits whet.

38

THEN in seemly style they searchingly inquired,

Putting to the prince private questions,

So that he courteously conceded he came of that court

Where high-souled Arthur held sway alone,

Ruler most royal of the Round Table;

And that Sir Gawain himself now sat in the house,

Having come that Christmas, by course of fortune.

Loudly laughed the lord when he learned what knight

He had in his house; such happiness it brought

That all the men within the moat made merry,

And promptly appeared in the presence of Gawain,

To whose person are proper all prowess and worth,

And pure and perfect manners, and praises unceasing.

道道美味可口,高文吃得十分满意。
善良的骑士称这顿饭为一次盛宴,
但在一旁作陪的仆人却
　　说话两样:
　　"这回没能让你开荤,[18]
　　但苦日子很快过完。"
　　骑士心里喜不自胜,
　　美酒已使他飘飘然。

38

然后他们用得体的口吻询问,
向优秀的骑士提了一些问题。
高文谦逊地说出自己的身份,
承认自己来自高尚的亚瑟宫廷,
来自圆桌骑士最光荣的首领身边。
他还说自己这次来到这里,
恰好碰上圣诞节,纯属命运的安排。
当城堡主知道他是何人后,
开心地哈哈大笑;此事一传开,
整座城堡都充满了欢乐,
大伙立即来到高文跟前,
连声称赞他,说他为人勇敢而高尚,
他的风范纯洁而完美。

His reputation rates first in the ranks of men.

Each knight neared his neighbour and softly said,

"Now we shall see displayed the seemliest manners

And the faultless figures of virtuous discourse.

Without asking we may hear how to hold conversation

Since we have seized upon this scion of good breeding.

God has given us of his grace good measure

In granting us such a guest as Gawain is,

When, contented at Christ's birth, the courtiers shall sit

   And sing.

  This noble knight will prove

  What manners the mighty bring;

  His converse of courtly love

  Shall spur our studying."

39

WHEN the fine man had finished his food and risen.

It was nigh and near to the night's mid-hour.

Priests to their prayers paced their way

And rang the bells royally, as rightly they should,

To honour that high feast with evensong.

The lord inclines to prayer, the lady too;

Into her private pew she prettily walks;

在众人心目中,他的声望即刻上升,
骑士们凑在一起,小声地议论:
"这下我们可有机会见识见识
什么行为够气派,什么人算完美,
既然巧遇了这位血统高贵的人,
我们就可以将他的谈话亲耳聆听。
能见到高文这样一位来宾,
那是上帝有意让我们评判他的品行,
在基督的诞辰,大家济济一堂,

   开心地歌唱。

  高尚的骑士将证明:

  他具有什么样的派头,

  等他谈起宫廷的爱情,

  我们还可向他学两手。"

39

当这位好人儿吃饱肚子站起,
时间已接近白昼与黑夜的交界,
牧师按部就班开读祈祷文,
尽心尽职敲响了钟声,
严肃的晚祷使盛宴平添几分荣耀。
主人和他夫人一道参加这次仪式,
那女子风度翩翩走进她的专座,

Gawain advances gaily and goes there quickly,

But the lord gripped his gown and guided him to his seat,

Acknowledged him by name and benevolently said

In the whole world he was the most welcome of men.

Gawain spoke his gratitude, they gravely embraced,

And sat in serious mood the whole service through.

Then the lady had a longing to look on the knight;

With her bevy of beauties she abandoned her pew.

Most beautiful of body and bright of complexion,

Most winsome in ways of all women alive,

She seemed to Sir Gawain, excelling Guinevere.

To squire that splendid dame, he strode through the chancel.

Another lady led her by the left hand,

A matron, much older, past middle age,

Who was highly honoured by an escort of squires.

Most unlike to look on those ladies were,

For if the one was winsome, then withered was the other.

Hues rich and rubious were arrayed on the one,

Rough wrinkles on the other rutted the cheeks.

Kerchiefed with clear pearls clustering was the one,

Her breast and bright throat bare to the sight,

Shining like sheen of snow shed on the hills;

The other was swathed with a wimple wound to the throat

And choking her swarthy chin in chalk-white veils.

On her forehead were folded enveloping silks,

高文兴致勃勃,快步跟进。

主人抓住他的衣襟,为他指引,

招呼他的名字,并和蔼地说,

他是世界上最受欢迎的人。

高文向他表示感谢,两人热烈拥抱,

然后一本正经坐下,直到仪式结束。

这时,女主人想过来见见骑士,

她与一班美人儿从座位上站起;

这位夫人花容月貌,身姿优美,

比世上其他所有女子都更迷人,

在高文眼里,她甚至胜过奎妮佛几分。

绝色佳人穿过圣坛,走向高文。

另有一位女士挽着她的左手,

那是位年纪较大的妇人,已逾中年,

在大家的陪衬下,女主人更显高贵。

她的姿容确实与众不同,

因她太迷人,老夫人显得十分寒碜。

只因千娇百媚集于她一身,

老妇人的脸让人觉得只有皱纹。

她的头巾装饰着明珠串串,

她的酥胸和脖颈十分招惹人眼,

白白净净的犹如山上的积雪浏亮晶莹。

另一位的脖子上也系了块头巾,

那模样好像黝黑下巴上缠了上吊用的白绫。

女主人头上还佩有绫罗头饰,

Trellised about with trefoils and tiny rings.

Nothing was bare on that beldame but the black brows,

The two eyes, protruding nose and stark lips,

And those were a sorry sight and exceedingly bleary:

A grand lady, God knows, of greatness in the world

Well tried!

Her body was stumpy and squat,

Her buttocks bulging and wide;

More pleasure a man could plot

With the sweet one at her side.

40

WHEN Gawain had gazed on that gracious-looking creature

He gained leave of the lord to go along with the ladies.

He saluted the senior, sweeping a low bow,

But briefly embraced the beautiful one,

Kissing her in courtly style and complimenting her.

They craved his acquaintance and he quickly requested

To be their faithful follower, if they would so favour him.

They took him between them, and talking, they led him

To a high room. By the hearth they asked first

For spices, which unstintingly men sped to bring,

And always with heart-warming, heady wine.

上面琳琅满目尽是珠光宝气。

那老太婆头上却什么也没有，

除了那黑眉、双眼、大鼻和干瘪的嘴唇，

她的姿容暗淡无光，见之令人失望。

上帝知道，女主人在这艰难人世堪称——

国色天香！

老妇人却是又矮又粗，

那臀部更是宽而无当，

她身边偏偏有一佳丽，

这对比让人更觉愉悦。

40

高文看见这风仪秀整的尤物，

便离开主人向那班女子走过去。

他先向那位年长的深深鞠躬，

然后轻轻地拥抱这位美人，

按宫廷礼节吻了她，称赞她的美貌。

她们很愿意认识他，骑士则马上恳求

她们垂青，让他做忠实的侍从。

她们于是挽着他，说笑着走进另一间屋子。

在炉边坐定后，她们吩咐备下饮料，

此事仆人们办得十分爽利，

令人陶醉的美酒不断送上来。

In lovingkindness the lord leaped up repeatedly

And many times reminded them that mirth should flow;

Elaborately lifted up his hood, looped it on a spear,

And offered it as a mark of honour to whoever should prove able

To make the most mirth that merry Yuletide.

"And I shall essay, I swear, to strive with the best

Before this garment goes from me, by my good friends' help."

So with his mirth the mighty lord made thing merry

To gladden Sir Gawain with games in hall

     That night;

   Until, the time being spent,

   The lord demanded light.

   Gawain took his leave and went

   To rest in rare delight.

41

ON that morning when men call to mind the birth

Of our dear Lord born to die for our destiny,

Joy waxes in dwellings the world over for his sake:

And so it befell there on the feast day with fine fare.

Both at main meals and minor repasts strong men served

Rare dishes with fine dressings to the dais company.

Highest, in the place of honour, the ancient crone sat,

慷慨的主人来来回回忙个不停，

一次次提醒大家要玩得尽兴。

他优雅地将自己的长袍挂到一支长矛上，

许诺谁能在圣诞之夜制造至高的欢乐，

就可以得到这件象征荣誉的长袍。

"我发誓，在它从我这里被人取走以前，

只要朋友帮忙，我自己也要争做快乐王子。"

就这样，强健的主人使城堡充满欢乐，

圣诞之夜各种游戏使高文

　　　　称心可意。

　　　时间不知不觉过去，

　　　主人吩咐掌灯照明，

　　　高文于是向他告辞，

　　　欢欢喜喜上床安寝。

41

第二天早晨，人们思念主的降生，

他的生与死全为人类的命运，

为了纪念他，全世界喜悦欢腾，

盛大的庆祝宴乐就在这天举行。

无论主餐或小饮，大家都身着盛装，

围坐一起将稀有的美食品尝。

我相信，那老太婆坐了首席，

And the lord, so I believe, politely next.

Together sat Gawain and the gay lady

In mid-table, where the meal was mannerly served first;

And after throughout the hall, as was held best,

Each gallant by degree was graciously served.

There was meat and merry-making and much delight,

To such an extent that it would try me to tell of it,

Even if perhaps I made the effort to describe it.

But yet I know the knight and the nobly pretty one

Found such solace and satisfaction seated together,

In the discreet confidences of their courtly dalliance,

Their irreproachably pure and polished repartee,

That with princes' sport their play of wit surpassingly

      Compares.

    Pipes and side-drums sound,

    Trumpets entune their airs;

    Each soul its solace found,

    And the two were enthralled with theirs.

42

THAT day they made much merriment, and on the morrow again,

And thickly the joys thronged on the third day after;

But gentle was the jubilation on St John's Day,

接下去是彬彬有礼的男主人，
高文与那快活的夫人坐中间，
每道菜都先端到他们面前。
然后，在济济一堂的大厅里，
每位宾客各按名分受到款待。
宴席上美食丰盛，大家其乐融融，
那场面我即使竭力描写，
也难道其盛况之万一。
但我知道骑士和美人坐在一起，
两人都感到欣慰和满意，
他们含而不露地调情，
妙语滴水不漏，高贵而文雅，
他们的机智足以使明君圣主
　　　相形见绌。
　　笛声鼓声响成一片，
　　喇叭阵阵回荡大厅；
　　每位宾客称心如意，
　　英雄美人相互爱慕。

42

那天他们玩得尽兴，第二天也一样，
第三天圣约翰节快活依然，
但这天的狂欢最让人留恋，

The final one for feasting, so the folk there thought.

As there were guests geared to go in the grey dawn

They watched the night out with wine in wonderful style,

Leaping night-long in their lordly dances.

At last when it was late those who lived far off,

Each one, bid farewell before wending their ways.

Gawain also said goodbye, but the good host grasped him,

Led him to the hearth of his own chamber,

And held him back hard, heartily thanking him

For the fine favour he had manifested to him.

In honouring his house that high feast-tide,

Brightening his abode with his brilliant company:

"As long as I live, sir, I believe I shall thrive

Now Gawain has been my guest at God's own feast."

"Great thanks, sir," said Gawain. "In good faith, yours,

All yours is the honour, may the High King requite it!

I stand at your service, knight, to satisfy your will

As good use engages me, in great things and small,

      By right."

    The lord then bid his best

    Longer to delay the knight,

    But Gawain, replying, pressed

    His departure in all despite.

大家知道,那是宴庆的最后一天。

许多宾客次日一早要起程,

他们于是尽情地开怀畅饮,

用贵族的舞蹈来打发长夜。

最后,时候不早,路远的宾客

一一告辞,然后登程上路。

高文也想道别,但主人拉住他的手

把他带进自己的卧室,

他执意挽留他,并表示衷心感谢,

感谢他一片至诚美意,

圣诞佳节光临他的城池,

高文的到来使这里蓬荜生辉。

"爵士,有你在上帝的节日做我的客人,

我相信,我今后的日子必定一帆风顺。"

"谢谢你,阁下,"高文说,"说句实话,

信感荣幸的是我,但愿主报答你!

我将随时为你效劳,听从你的召唤,

就像此刻我有事在身,无论如何

　　　要去完成。"

　　主人一个劲挽留,

　　想让他多住几天;

　　但高文初衷不改,

　　无论如何要辞行。

43

THEN with courteous inquiry the castellan asked

What fierce exploit had sent him forth, at that festive season,

From the King's court at Camelot, so quickly and alone,

Before the holy time was over in the homes of men.

"You may in truth well demand," admitted the knight.

"A high and urgent errand hastened me from thence,

For I myself am summoned to seek out a place

To find which I know not where in the world to look.

For all the land in Logres—may our Lord help me!

I would not fail to find it on the feast of New Year.

So this is my suit, sir, which I beseech of you here,

That you tell me in truth if tale ever reached you

Of the Green Chapel, or what ground or glebe it stands on,

Or of the knight who holds it, whose hue is green.

For at that place I am pledged, by the pact between us,

To meet that man, if I remain alive.

From now until the New Year is not a great time,

And if God will grant it me, more gladly would I see him

Than gain any good possession, by God's son!

I must wend my way, with your good will, therefore;

I am reduced to three days in which to do my business,

43

然后城堡主人彬彬有礼地询问,

是什么重大使命促使他圣诞节外出,

孤身一人离开凯姆洛特王宫,

害得神圣的节日也未能在家安度。

"你问得正好,"骑士回答,

"确实有重大使命促使我外出。

有人要我前去寻找一个处所,

但我却不知道它到底在哪里。

愿主帮助我! 让我在新年佳节这天

能在罗格里^[19]一带找到这个所在。

阁下,在此我要请求你如实告诉我,

你是否听说过绿色教堂,

是否知道它位于何方,

或者听说有位绿衣骑士占据该地。

根据我们间所立的誓约,

我只要活着,就要去那里会他。

现在离新年已经不远,

只要上帝眷顾,我宁愿失去一切,

也要见到此人,基督可以为我做证!

谢谢你一片好意,但我必须上路,

我的期限已经只剩三天,

And I think it fitter to fall dead than fail in my errand."

Then the lord said laughingly, "You may linger a while,

For I shall tell you where your tryst is by your term's end.

Give yourself no more grief for the Green Chapel's whereabouts,

For you may lie back in your bed, brave man, at ease

Till full morning on the First, and then fare forth

To the meeting place at mid-morning to manage how you may

   Out there.

  Leave not till New Year's Day,

  Then get up and go with cheer;

  You shall be shown the way;

  It is hardly two miles from here."

44

THEN Gawain was glad and gleefully exclaimed,

"Now above all, most heartily do I offer you thanks!

For my goal is now gained, and by grace of yours

I shall dwell here and do what you deem good for me."

So the lord seized Sir Gawain, seated him beside himself,

And to enliven their delight, he had the ladies fetched,

And much gentle merriment they long made together.

The lord, as one like to take leave of his senses

And not aware of what he was doing, spoke warmly and merrily.

不达目的,我死不甘心!"

主人听后哈哈大笑,"你不妨再住几天,
期限以前,我会告诉你约会的地点。
用不着再为找不着绿色教堂发愁,
好壮士,你尽管放心在这里休息,
直到元旦上午再出发去那里,
我担保你午前赶到,以后的事就——
　　　全凭你自己。
　　请你务必等到岁初,
　　然后欢欢喜喜出发;
　　那时有人给你带路,
　　此去二英里即可抵达。"

44

高文满心欢喜,他对城堡主说,
"我向你表示最诚挚的谢意!
我已达到目的,承蒙你一片盛情,
我要住在这里,享受美好的一切。"
主人于是拉着高文,让他坐在自己身边,
他还叫来小姐夫人陪伴助兴,
两人在一起消受了许多欢乐。
城堡主说话既热情又开心,
像个动了疯劲的人不知厉害轻重。

Then he spoke to Sir Gawain, saying out loud,

"You have determined to do the deed I ask:

Will you hold to your undertaking here and now?"

"Yes, sir, in good sooth," said the true knight,

"While I stay in your stronghold, I shall stand at your command."

"Since you have spurred," the lord said, "from afar,

Then watched awake with me, you are not well supplied

With either sustenance or sleep, for certain, I know;

So you shall lie long in your room, late and at ease

Tomorrow till the time of mass, and then take your meal

When you will, with my wife beside you

To comfort you with her company till I come back to court.

   You stay,

  And I shall get up at dawn.

  I will to the hunt away."

  When Gawain's agreement was sworn

  He bowed, as brave knights may.

45

"MOREOVER," said the man, "Let us make a bargain

That whatever I win in the woods be yours,

And any achievement you chance on here, you exchange for it.

Sweet sir, truly swear to such a bartering,

这一回他就大声地对高文说：
"你已说过要照我的话去做，
如今还想不遵守自己的诺言？"
"当然，阁下，"诚实的高文回答，
"只要我在城堡一天，我随时听从差遣。"
主人说："你大老远骑马来到这儿，
据我观察，你一路上显然没有吃好，
没有睡好，这一点我当然知道；
因此，明天你可以在房里多睡觉，
舒舒服服一直躺到做弥撒，
什么时候用餐悉听尊便，
我留下夫人陪伴你，安慰你，直到我——
　　　　返回城堡。
　　而我则一早就外出，
　　到森林里打围行猎。"
　　高文爵士表示同意，
　　主人行骑士礼致谢。

45

"还有，"主人说，"让我们来做一笔交易，
我在林中猎得的一切都归你，
作为交换，你则将这里所得的给我。
亲爱的爵士，请你为这桩买卖起个誓，

Whether fair fortune or foul befall from it."

"By God," said the good Gawain, "I agree to that,

And I am happy that you have an eye to sport."

Then the prince of that people said, "What pledge of wine

Is brought to seal the bargain?" And they burst out laughing.

They took drink and toyed in trifling talk,

These lords and ladies, as long as they liked.

And then with French refinement and many fair words

They stood, softly speaking, to say goodnight,

Kissing as they parted company in courtly style.

With lithe liege servants in plenty and lambent torches,

Each brave man was brought to his bed at last,

   Full soft.

  Before they fared to bed

  They rehearsed their bargain oft.

  That people's prince, men said,

  Could fly his wit aloft.

不管它对你是凶是吉。"

"上帝做证，"高文说，"我同意你的条件，

我很高兴能亲眼见见这样的游戏。"

然后众宾客说道："让我们多拿些

酒来庆祝这桩交易的达成。"他们哈哈大笑。

大伙于是喝了酒，接着又闲聊了一会。

最后男男女女一一站起，

自由自在围在一起交谈，

以法国式的派头和文绉绉的语言道安，

大大方方地亲吻分手。

在恭敬小心的仆役陪同下，

每个宾客照着火把被领进——

        舒适的卧房。

    他们上床就寝以前，

    继续议论那笔交易，

    他们都说城堡主人，

    办事情真有些离谱。

FIT III

46

IN the faint light before dawn folk were stirring;
Guests who had to go gave orders to their grooms,
Who busied themselves briskly with the beasts, saddling,
Trimming their tackle and tying on their luggage.
Arrayed for riding in the richest style,
Guests leaped on their mounts lightly, laid hold of their bridles,
And each rider rode out on his own chosen way.
The beloved lord of the land was not the last up,
Being arrayed for riding with his retinue in force.
He ate a sop hastily when he had heard mass,
And hurried with horn to the hunting field;
Before the sun's first rays fell on the earth,
On their high steeds were he and his knights.
Then these cunning hunters came to couple their hounds,
Cast open the kennel doors and called them out,
And blew on their bugles three bold notes.

第三章

46

东方刚发白，人们又忙碌起来，
准备上路的宾客使唤他们的听差，
让他们给马备好鞍辔；
听差们敏捷地给马上鞍，整理行装。
待骑马所需的一切拾掇停当，
客人们便飞身上马，紧握缰绳，
——踏上自己的行程。
尊敬的城堡主也一早起床，
与他的随从一起备好马鞍。
做完弥撒后，匆匆吃了些面包片，
然后就带上号角准备去狩猎的森林；
当太阳的光辉初照大地，
他与随行骑士都上了坐骑。
老练的猎手用绳子将猎狗拴住，
打开狗舍把狗一只只放出，
悠扬的号角顿时响成一片。

The hounds broke out barking, baying fiercely,

And when they went chasing, they were whipped back.

There were a hundred choice huntsmen there, whose fame

    Resounds.

    To their stations keepers strode;

    Huntsmen unleashed hounds:

    The forest overflowed

    With the strident bugle sounds.

47

AT the first cry wild creatures quivered with dread.

The deer in distraction darted down to the dales

Or up to the high ground, but eagerly they were

Driven back by the beaters, who bellowed lustily.

They let the harts with high-branching heads have their freedom,

And the brave bucks, too, with their broad antlers,

For the noble prince had expressly prohibited

Meddling with male deer in the months of close season.

But the hinds were held back with a "Hey" and a "Whoa!"

And does driven with much din to the deep valleys.

Lo! the arrows' slanting flight as they were loosed!

A shaft flew forth at every forest turning,

The broad head biting on the brown flank.

猎狗吠叫着,来势十分凶猛,

一旦离群乱窜,鞭子便抽打到它们背上。

猎手总共有一百光景,个个具有

        卓著的声名。

    猎场管理员各就其位,

    猎人们忙将猎狗释放,

    号角声阵阵何其尖锐,

    在林子上空久久回荡。

47

第一阵呐喊使野兽魂飞魄散,

受惊的鹿逃进山谷,窜上山冈,

但很快又被捕猎者赶回,

人喊犬吠,森林里喧闹非常。

他们放过长有大角的雄鹿,

高贵的城堡主曾有禁令下达:

在限制行猎的月份里,

碰上雄鹿一概不许捕杀。

但他们可以随意捕猎雌鹿,

高声吆喝着把它们赶向深谷。

看哪,那呼啸而出的箭飞得多快!

每个山窝都有箭杆在凌空飞越,

宽大的箭镞击中褐色的躯体,

They screamed as the blood streamed out, sank dead on the sward,

Always harried by hounds hard on their heels,

And the hurrying hunters' high horn notes.

Like the rending of ramped hills roared the din.

If one of the wild beasts slipped away from the archers

It was dragged down and met death at the dog-bases

After being hunted from the high ground and harried to the water,

So skilled were the hunt-servants at stations lower down,

So gigantic the greyhounds that grabbed them in a flash,

Seizing them savagely, as swift, I swear,

     As sight.

   The lord, in humour high

   Would spur, then stop and alight.

   In bliss the day went by

   Till dark drew on, and night.

48

THUS by the forest borders the brave lord sported,

And the good man Gawain, on his gay bed lying,

Lay hidden till the light of day gleamed on the walls,

Covered with fair canopy, the curtains closed,

And as in slumber he slept on, there slipped into his mind

A slight, suspicious sound, and the door stealthily opened.

猎物流着血,哀鸣着倒地死去,

它们身边围着凶猛的猎犬,

同时还有猎手的号角声阵阵逼近。

喧声如雷,似乎整座大山就要炸开。

野兽一旦被从山坡驱逐到溪水边,

即便逃脱了弓箭手的射击,

也难免被成群的猎狗缠住丢了性命,

狩猎场里的猎手射技高超无比,

猎狗捕捉猎物那么敏捷,那么凶猛,

我敢打赌,那速度——

迅如闪电。

那城堡主神采奕奕,

马上马下忙个不停。

欢天喜地一天过去,

直到黑夜悄悄降临。

48

就这样,城堡主在森林里行猎,

而好人儿高文却躺在床上,

掩身于床罩下、帐子里,

直到白昼的阳光照见城墙。

睡眼蒙眬中,突然有一声音传到他耳里,

轻微而可疑,卧室的门随之悄然开启。

He raised up his head out of the bedclothes,

Caught up the corner of the curtain a little

And watched warily towards it, to see what it was.

It was the lady, loveliest to look upon,

Who secretly and silently secured the door,

Then bore towards his bed: the brave knight, embarrassed,

Lay flat with fine adroitness and feigned sleep.

Silently she stepped on, stole to his bed,

Caught up the curtain, crept within,

And seated herself softly on the side of the bed.

There she watched a long while, waiting for him to wake.

Slyly close this long while lay the knight,

Considering in his soul this circumstance,

Its sense and likely sequel, for it seemed marvellous.

"Still, it would be more circumspect," he said to himself,

"To speak and discover her desire in due course."

So he stirred and stretched himself, twisting towards her,

Opened his eyes and acted as if astounded;

And, to seem the safer by such service, crossed himself

      In dread.

    With chin and cheek so fair,

    White ranged with rosy red,

    With laughing lips, and air

    Of love, she lightly said:

他从床上微微抬起头，

并将帐子一角悄悄拉起，

警惕地张望着，想看个究竟。

来者是女主人，看上去十分漂亮，

进来后她随手将门轻轻关上，

然后朝他走来：这使骑士十分尴尬，

他赶紧挺直身子，假装睡着。

她不声不响来到他的床前，

拉起罗帷，探进身子，

然后便在床沿下悄悄坐下。

她观察了好一会，等待他醒来。

骑士躺得离她很近，

心里一边思考发生的事情，

总觉得有点不可思议。

他对自己说："为了慎重起见，

我最好先弄清她的来意。"

于是他翻身把脸朝向她，

睁开眼，装出十分惊讶；

为防不测他还惶惶地在胸前

　　　画了十字。

　　她白嫩娟秀的脸蛋，

　　顿时泛起一阵红晕，

　　嘴唇翕动微露笑口，

　　那声音轻柔而多情。

49

"GOOD morning, Sir Gawain," the gay one murmured,

"How unsafely you sleep, that one may slip in here!

Now you are taken in a trice. Unless a truce come between us,

I shall bind you to your bed—of that be sure."

The lady uttered laughingly those playful words.

"Good morning, gay lady," Gawain blithely greeted her.

"Do with me as you will: that well pleases me.

For I surrender speedily and sue for grace,

Which, to my mind, since I must, is much the best course,"

And thus he repaid her with repartee and ready laughter.

"But if, lovely lady, your leave were forthcoming,

And you were pleased to free your prisoner and pray him to rise,

I would abandon my bed for a better habiliment,

And have more happiness in our honey talk."

"Nay, verily, fine sir," urged the voice of that sweet one,

"You shall not budge from your bed. I have a better idea.

I shall hold you fast here on this other side as well

And so chat on with the chevalier my chains have caught.

For I know well, my knight, that your name is Sir Gawain,

Whom all the world worships, wherever he ride;

For lords and their ladies, and all living folk,

49

"早上好,高文爵士,"美人儿低声说,

"看你睡得多不安全,竟然让人溜进来!

如果敌我交战,你马上将束手就擒,

我可以把你绑在床上——这可以肯定。"

女主人边笑边说这番戏言。

"早上好,美丽的太太,"高文快活地说。

"就照你说的办吧,那倒真让人开心,

我随时准备追求美,并向它屈服,

即使是强迫,对我也是天大的乐事。"

他一边笑一边巧妙地回答。

"可爱的太太,但你得马上离开一会,

你一定乐意让你的俘虏起床,

而我也必须起来换上更体面的服装,

那时我们可以更愉快地交谈。"

"不,好先生,"悦耳的声音急切地说,

"你不应离开你的眠床。我有更好的主意:

既然我的锁链套住了一位武士,

我就要紧紧握住链子的一端。

我知道,骑士,你的大名叫高文,

不管你到哪里,全世界都崇敬你,

不管男人女子,只要是活着的人,

Hold your lonour in high esteem, and your courtesy.

And now—here you are truly, and we are utterly alone;

My lord and his liegemen are a long way off;

Others still bide in their beds, my bower-maidens too;

Shut fast and firmly with a fine hasp is the door;

And since I have in this house him who pleases all,

As long as my time lasts I shall lingering in talk take

My fill.

My young body is yours,

Do with it what you will;

My strong necessities force

Me to be your servant still."

50

"IN good truth," said Gawain, "that is a gain indeed,

Though I am hardly the hero of whom you speak,

To be held in such honour as you here suggest,

I am altogether unworthy, I own it freely.

By God, I should be glad, if you granted it right

For me to essay by speech or some other service,

To pleasure such a perfect lady—pure joy it would be."

"In good truth, Sir Gawain," the gay lady replied,

"If I slighted or set at naught your spotless fame

都仰慕你的荣名和风度。

如今你就在这里，而我们又单独在一起；

我的主人及其扈从已远远离开；

其他的人还没起床，包括我的随身女仆；

房门也已经用搭扣紧紧关上；

既然我已把人人喜欢的骑士扣留在此，

只要时间允许，我就要与他长叙，直到

   心满意足。

  我这青春之躯属于你，

  随你如何处置都行；

  做你的奴仆任凭驱驰，

  乃是我最大的心愿。"

50

"毫无疑问，"高文说，"这是我的福分，

尽管我并不是你言下那种英雄。

我完全不具备你所说的那份荣耀，

这一点我应该坦率地承认，

但如果你能通过什么法子加以证明，

上帝做证，那倒很称我的心。

能取悦你这样的女子，真是赏心乐事。"

"说句实话，爵士，"快活的女主人说，

"若我藐视你的荣名和勇敢，

And your all-pleasing prowess, it would show poor breeding.

But there is no lack of ladies who would love, noble one,

To hold you in their arms, as I have you here,

And linger in the luxury of your delightful discourse,

Which would perfectly pleasure them and appease their woes—

Rather than have riches or the red gold they own.

But as I love that Lord, the Celestial Ruler,

I have wholly in my hand what all desire

      Through his grace."

    Not loth was she to allure,

    This lady fair of face;

    But the knight with speeches pure

    Answered in each case.

51

"MADAM," said the merry man, "May Mary requite you!

For in good faith I have found in you free-hearted generosity.

Certain men for their deeds receive esteem from others,

But for myself, I do not deserve the respect they show me;

Your honourable mind makes you utter only what is good."

"Now by Mary," said the noble lady, "Not so it seems to me,

For were I worth the whole of womankind,

And all the wealth in the world were in my hand,

那只能说明我缺乏教养。
别的女人也会爱慕你，
把你抱在怀里，就像我对待你那样。
他们会恋恋不舍地与你促膝交谈，
与你相伴能让人快活、减轻痛苦，
拥有财富和黄金不如拥有你。
我热爱主，那天上的统治者，
蒙主厚爱，别人渴求的一切我这里
　　　应有尽有。"

　　这位风致韵绝的女子，
　　一心一意要引诱高文，
　　但骑士用巧妙的言辞，
　　使她一次次不能得逞。

51

"夫人，"高文说，"愿圣母保佑你！
我发现你为人坦诚而大方。
别的男子因建过功勋而受人尊敬，
而我却不值得人们的敬仰；
你心灵高尚，只会将美好的事物颂扬。"
"圣母做证，"夫人说，"我不是那种人，
我具有一个女性所具有的一切，
世上的财富我一点也不缺，

And if bargaining I were to bid to bring my self a lord—

With your noble qualities, knight, made known to me now,

Your good looks, gracious manner and great courtesy,

All of which I have heard of before, but here prove true—

No lord that is living could be allowed to excel you."

"Indeed, dear lady, you did better," said the knight,

"But I am proud of the precious price you put on me,

And solemnly as your servant say you are my sovereign.

May Christ requite it you: I have become your knight."

Then of many matters they talked till mid-morning and after,

And all the time she behaved as if she adored him;

But Sir Gawain was on guard in a gracious manner.

Though she was the winsomest woman the warrior had known,

He was less love-laden because of the loss the must

     Now face—

  His destruction by the stroke,

  For come it must was the case.

  The lady of leaving then spoke;

  He assented with speedy grace.

52

THEN she gave him goodbye, glinting with laughter,

And standing up, astounded him with these strong words:

如果让自己选择一位夫婿，

骑士，我会选择具有你这样品质的人，

我已了解你，包括外貌、风度和谦逊的品格，

先前就曾听说，这次得到证明；

世上活着的人谁也不能与你相比。"

"夫人，你已做过更好的选择，"骑士说，

"但你盛情的赞美，我仍然引以为荣，

我要像仆人那样认真地说：你是我的主子，

愿基督保佑你，我已成为你的骑士。"

就这样，他们海阔天空几乎谈了一上午，

她的一言一行好像都在证明她的钟情；

而高文却潇洒大方，一直保持警觉。

尽管她是他见过最迷人的女子，

但他仍不受爱情所累，因为他必须面临

　　砍头考验。

　　那一斧将导致他毁灭，

　　而且事情必然要发生。

　　女主人终于起身告辞，

　　高文即刻大方地应允。

52

她一笑百媚生，向高文道别，

但起身时所说的话令人好不惊讶：

"May He who prospers every speech for this pleasure reward you!
I cannot bring myself to believe that you could be Gawain."
"How so?" said the knight, speaking urgently,
For he feared he had failed to observe the forms of courtesy.
But the beauteous one blessed him and brought out this argument:
"Such a great man as Gawain is granted to be,
The very vessel of virtue and fine courtesy,
Could scarcely have stayed such a sojourn with a lady
Without craving a kiss out of courtesy,
Touched by some trifling hint at the tail-end of a speech."
"So be it, as you say," then said Gawain,
"I shall kiss at your command, as becomes a knight
Who fears to offend you; no further plea is needed."
Whereupon she approached him, and penned him in her arms,
Leaned over him lovingly and gave the lord a kiss.
Then they commended each other to Christ in comely style,
And without more words she went out by the door.
He made ready to rise with rapid haste,
Summoned his servant, selected his garb,
And walked down, when he was dressed, debonairly to mass.
Then he went to the well-served meal which awaited him,
And made merry sport till the moon rose
      At night.
   Never was baron bold
   So taken by ladies bright,

"愿有求必应的上帝奖赏你!
我不敢相信你真的就是那位高文爵士。"
"这话这么说？"骑士急切地问,
他担心自己有什么地方失了礼。
美人儿祝福他,说出这样一番话:
"像高文这样一个伟大的人,
理所当然是道德与礼义的典范,
他与一位女子交谈了大半天,
临别时哪怕只有小小的暗示,
也不会忘记给对方一个礼节性的吻。"
"那就照你的意思做吧,"高文说,
"只要不失骑士之礼,我就遵命吻你,
我只怕冒犯你,不敢指望太多。"
她于是靠上前去,将他抱在怀里,
亲热地依偎着他,给了他一个吻。
他们还用得体的语言相互祝福,
这之后她默默走出了房间。
高文随后赶紧从床上爬起,
唤过仆役,取过他的衣服,
穿上后欢欢喜喜去做弥撒,
享用特意为他准备的丰盛酒食,
余下的时间他便在城堡消遣,直到
　　　　月亮升起。
　　　从前从没有哪位贵人,
　　　受到美人儿如此关怀,

That young one and the old:
They throve all three in delight.

53

AND still at his sport spurred the castellan,
Hunting the barren hinds in holt and on heath.
So many had he slain, by the setting of the sun,
Of does and other deer, that it was downright wonderful.
Then at the finish the folk flocked in eagerly,
And quickly collected the killed deer in a heap.
Those highest in rank came up with hosts of attendants,
Picked out what appeared to be the plumpest beasts
And, according to custom, had them cut open with finesse.
Some who ceremoniously assessed them there
Found two fingers' breadth of fat on the worst.
Then they slit open the slot, seized the first stomach,
Scraped it with a keen knife and tied up the tripes.
Next they hacked off all the legs, the hide was stripped,
The belly broken open and the bowels removed
Carefully, lest they loosen the ligature of the knot.
Then they gripped the gullet, disengaged deftly
The wezand from the windpipe and whipped out the guts.
Then their sharp knives shore through the shoulder-bones,

那一老一少再加高文，

这一天过得逍遥自在。

53

再说那位城堡主催马扬鞭

在山丘冈峦捕猎愚昧的鹿群。

太阳尚未下山，他们已射杀许多头鹿，

这一天的收获十分可观！

最后他们集合到一块，

很快把猎物堆成一堆。

几位德高望重的猎手带着助手过来，

挑选出其中最肥最壮的鹿，

按老规矩将它们一一宰杀。

有人还在一旁认真地估价，

发现最瘦的一头也有二指厚的脂肪。

然后他们剖开鹿的胸腔，

用锋利的刀割下胃囊，并用绳子扎紧，

接着剁下鹿腿，剥去鹿皮，

小心翼翼地破腹取肠，

留意不让打结的地方松散。

他们还卡住鹿的咽喉，拔去食管，

飞快地清除所有的内脏。

锋利的刀刃插进胛骨，

Which they slid out of a small hole, leaving the sides intact.

Then they cleft the chest clean through, cutting it in two.

Then again at the gullet a man began to work

And straight away rived it, right to the fork,

Flicked out the shoulder-fillets, and faithfully then

He rapidly ripped free the rib-fillets.

Similarly, as is seemly, the spine was cleared

All the way to the haunch, which hung from it;

And they heaved up the whole haunch and hewed it off;

And that is called, according to its kind, the numbles,

   I find.

  At the thigh-forks then they strain

  And free the folds behind,

  Hurrying to hack all in twain,

  The backbone to unbind.

54

THEN they hewed off the head and also the neck,

And after sundered the sides swiftly from the chine,

And into the foliage they flung the fee of the raven.

Then each fellow, for his fee, as it fell to him to have,

Skewered through the stout flanks beside the ribs,

And then by the hocks of the haunches they hung up their booty.

从一个小口子穿出,使两肋丝毫未损。

他们接着将胸腔剖开,一分为二。

一位屠夫随后从喉部下手,

顺着脊骨一直分解到下肢,

前腿部分首先被切割离体,

两肋转眼间也分割成一段段肉条。

就这样,脊骨两侧很快被削割干净,

最后只剩一个臀部连脊柱,

他们将这整个臀部割下来,

按照宰鹿人的行话,这一部分

    称为"下脚货"。

  他们然后拉紧两股,

  将弯曲的关节扳直,

  一分为二分割胯部,

  再将脊梁一一肢解。

54

然后他们砍下鹿的头和颈,

将脊椎两侧残剩的肉剁碎,

把它们抛进灌木丛作为乌鸦之食。

每个人都获得自己的一份报酬,

他们用串针将大块的肋条串起,

然后再将战利品挂上钩子。

On one of the finest fells they fed their hounds,
And let them have the lights, the liver and the tripes,
With bread well imbrued with blood mixed with them.
Boldly they blew the kill amid the baying of hounds.
Then off they went homewards, holding their meat,
Stalwartly sounding many stout horn-calls.
As dark was descending, they were drawing near
To the comely castle where quietly our knight stayed.

> Fires roared,
> And blithely hearts were beating
> As into hall came the lord.
> When Gawain gave him greeting,
> Joy abounded at the board.

55

THEN the master commanded everyone to meet in the hall,
Called the ladies to come down with their company of maidens.
Before all the folk on the floor, he bid men
Fetch the venison and place it before him.
Then gaily and in good humour to Gawain he called,
Told over the tally of the sturdy beasts,
And showed him the fine fat flesh flayed from the ribs.
'How does the sport please you? Do you praise me for it?

在一片美丽的山坡上,他们喂食猎犬,

让它们吃猎物的肺、肝和其他内脏,

以及一些沾了血污的面包。

狗吠声中,他们将自己的战果夸耀。

随着阵阵洪亮的号角声,

他们扛着鹿肉返回家门。

夜幕降临,他们来到城堡附近;

而我们的骑士则安安静静

　　　　度过这天。

　　当城堡主进入大厅,

　　炉火生旺,群情高昂。

　　高文过来与他见面,

　　厅堂上下喜气洋洋。

55

主人传令大家都到厅堂集合,

吩咐夫人及其女仆也全部下楼。

大伙尚未到齐,他又吩咐仆人

把鹿肉抬上来,放在他面前。

然后他兴致勃勃唤过高文,

让他过目猎物的数量,

给他看鹿肉上那层厚厚的脂肪。

"你觉得这次狩猎如何?你要不要赞扬我?

Am I thoroughly thanked for thriving as a huntsman?"

"Certainly," said the other, "Such splendid spoils

Have I not seen for seven years in the season of winter."

"And I give you all, Gawain," said the good man then,

"For according to our covenant you may claim it as your own."

"Certes, that is so, and I say the same to you,"

Said Gawain, "For my true gains in this great house,

I am not loth to allow, must belong to you."

And he put his arms round his handsome neck, hugging him,

And kissed him in the comeliest way he could think of.

"Accept my takings, sir, for I received no more;

Gladly would I grant them, however great they were."

"And therefore I thank you," the thane said, "Good!

Yours may be the better gift, if you would break it to me

Where your wisdom won you wealth of that kind."

"No such clause in our contract! Request nothing else!"

Said the other, "You have your due: ask more,

     None should."

    They laughed in blithe assent

    With worthy words and good;

    Then to supper they swiftly went,

    To fresh delicious food.

作为一名猎手，我是否可以自我夸耀一番？"

"当然可以，"高文说，"在这冬季，

我已有七年没见过这么多的战利品。"

"我把它全给你，高文，"好人儿说，

"按照我们的契约，这些全归你。"

"不错，我与你有约在先，"

高文说，"我在这屋里所得的一切，

也必须痛痛快快地交给你。"

他于是搭着肩膀拥抱骑士，

以高雅的姿势给了他一个吻。

"骑士，请你收下，这是我全部所得；

但不管收获多少，我全都交给你。"

"我要谢谢你，"城堡主说，"这太好了！

你凭智慧获得这样的财富，

并甘愿交给我，这礼物不轻。"

"契约上没有这样的条款，"高文说，

"你已经得到应得的一切，再想多得，

也是徒劳。"

两人说话友好亲近，

哈哈大笑意足心满，

然后快步离开大厅，

一道享用可口晚餐。

56

AND sitting afterwards by the hearth of an audience chamber,

Where retainers repeatedly brought them rare wines,

In their jolly jesting they jointly agreed

On a settlement similar to the preceding one;

To exchange the chance achievements of the morrow,

No matter how novel they were, at night when they met.

They accorded on this compact, the whole court observing,

And the bumper was brought forth in banter to seal it.

And at last they lovingly took leave of each other,

Each man hastening thereafter to his bed.

The cock having crowed and called only thrice,

The lord leaped from bed, and his liegemen too,

So that mass and a meal were meetly dealt with,

And by first light the folk to the forest were bound

       For the chase.

    Proudly the hunt with horns

    Soon drove through a desert place:

    Uncoupled through the thorns

    The great hounds pressed apace.

56

不久他们在客厅的炉膛旁坐下，
仆人们频频送上各种美酒，
欢声笑语中两人再次达成协议，
一致同意采取先前的法子：
第二天不管有什么新奇的收获，
晚上见面时一概悉数交换。
他们立下这份契约，众人亲眼所见，
戏谑中他们还干杯庆贺誓约立成。
最后两人十分友好地道过晚安，
各自匆匆回到自己的卧房。
当公鸡喔喔啼叫到三遍，
主人和他的随从马上起床，
接着按部就班做弥撒进早餐，
晨曦初上时，他们又去了森林
　　　　打围行猎。
　　猎队持号角豪气十足，
　　很快穿过一片蛮荒，
　　高大的猎犬钻越荆棘，
　　飞快地奔走在山冈上。

By a quagmire they quickly scented quarry and gave tongue,

And the chief huntsman ugred on the first hounds up,

Spurring them on with a splendid spate of words.

The hounds, hearing it, hurried there at once,

Fell on the trial furiously, forty together,

And made such echoing uproar, all howling at once,

That the rocky banks round about rang with the din.

Hunters inspirited them with sound of speech and horn.

Then together in a group, across the ground they surged

At speed between a pool and a spiteful crag.

On a stony knoll by a steep cliff at the side of a bog,

Where rugged rocks had roughly tumbled down,

They careered on the quest, the cry following,

Then surrounded the crag and the rocky knoll as well,

Certain their prey skulked inside their ring,

For the baying of the bloodhounds meant the beast was there.

Then they beat upon the bushes and bade him come out,

And he swung out savagely aslant the line of men,

A baneful boar of unbelievable size,

A solitary long since sundered from the herd,

Being old and brawny, the biggest of them all,

57

猎犬在沼泽地闻到气味开始狂吠，
领头的猎手把第一批猎犬放出，
不断用吆喝声催促它们奋勇上前，
猎犬闻声而动，迅速扑过去，
齐心协力向猎物发动凶猛的进攻，
四十只猎犬同时吠叫，其声如雷，
四周的岩壁也被震得叮叮有声。
猎手们用喊声、号角声激励猎犬。
猎犬则凑成一群，以飞快的速度
越过深潭和险峻的峭壁。
沼泽地旁有一片岩石众多的山坡，
那里嶙峋的怪石陡然向下延伸，
猎犬追踪至此，汪汪叫个不停，
它们把那片峭壁和山坡围住，
那猎物显然就藏匿在那里面，
猛犬的吠叫正是野兽存在的证明。
猎犬搜索树丛，将猎物从里面赶出，
那野兽疯狂地从猎手队列的一侧蹿出，
那是一头硕大无朋的公野猪！
它长期脱离自己的群体，
又老又壮，堪称同类中的魁首，

And grim and ghastly when he grunted: great was the grief
When he thrust through the hounds, hurling three to earth,
And sped on scot-free, swift and unscathed.
They hallooed, yelled, "Look out!" cried, "Hey, we have him!"
And blew horns boldly, to bring the bloodhounds together;
Many were the merry cries from men and dogs
As they hurried clamouring after their quarry to kill him on
       The track.
    Many times he turns at bay
    And tears the dogs which attack.
    He hurts the hounds, and they
    Moan in a piteous pack.

58

Then men shoved forward, shaped to shoot at him,
Loosed arrows at him, hitting him often,
But the points, for all their power, could not pierce his flanks,
Nor would the barbs bite on his bristling brow.
Though the smooth-shaven shaft shattered in pieces,
Wherever it hit, the head rebounded.
But when the boar was battered by blows unceasing,
Goaded and driven demented, he dashed at the men,
Striking them savagely as he assailed them in rushes,

它的咕噜声狰狞可怖:当它蹿过狗群,
竟连着拱翻三只狗,它自己却安然无恙,
那情景真有点惨不忍睹!
猎手们惊呼"当心!""我们看见了!"
他们赶紧吹响号角,将良犬召集起来;
人的吆喝、狗的狂吠响成一片,
他们呼啸着追踪猎物,一心要将它
          就地捕杀。
    野猪已经无路可走,
    它一次次回头反咬,
    那些被它咬伤的狗,
    在狗群中凄切哀号。

          58

猎手们争先恐后,开始向野猪射箭,
箭镞向它飞去,频频射中它的躯体,
尽管箭射得猛,却伤不了它的身,
箭镞上的倒钩刺不进长满鬃毛的额头。
光溜溜的箭杆被折断,
箭镞从它身上反弹回来。
野猪不断受到箭的进攻,
恼怒得发了狂,它冲向射手,
一路上凶狠地向他们乱拱乱咬,

So that some lacking stomach stood back in fear.

But the lord on a lithe horse lunged after him,

Blew on his bugle like a bold knight in battle,

Rallied the hounds as he rode through the rank thickets,

Pursuing this savage boar till the sun set.

And so they disported themselves this day

While our lovable lord lay in his bed.

At home the gracious Gawain in gorgeous clothes

     Reclined:

    The gay one did not forget

    To come with welcome kind,

    And early him beset

    To make him change his mind.

59

SHE came to the curtain and cast her eye

On Sir Gawain, who at once gave her gracious welcome,

And she answered him eagerly, with ardent words,

Sat at his side softly, and with a spurt of laughter

And a loving look, delivered these words:

"It seems to me strange, if, sir, you are Gawain,

A person so powerfully disposed to good,

Yet nevertheless know nothing of noble conventions,

胆小的人只好惶恐地向后逃避。
但城堡主却骑骏马冲上前去，
像战场上的骑士吹响号角，
一边穿过茂密的灌木，一边重新召集猎犬，
追击凶猛的野兽直到太阳下山。
这一天他们就在这样的消遣中度过，
而我们可爱的爵士却留在城堡，
身着华丽的睡衣悠闲地
　　　　斜靠在床上：
　　　那美人儿没有忘记，
　　　打扮漂亮前来拜访，
　　　为了让他改变主意，
　　　一大早就对他纠缠。

59

她进入帐帷，拿眼看着高文，
骑士即刻大大方方表示欢迎；
她则以十分热情的话回答，
一边轻轻地在床沿坐下，
带着迷人的眼神笑着对他说：
"我总觉得有点不合情理，爵士，
像你高文这样一个志趣高雅的人，
竟然会对高贵的礼节一无所知，

And when made aware of them, wave them away!

Quickly you have cast off what I schooled you in yesterday

By the truest of all tokens of talk I know of."

"What?" said the wondering knight, "I am not aware of one.

But if it be true what you tell, I am entirely to blame."

"I counselled you then about kissing," the comely one said;

"When a favour is conferred, it must be forthwith accepted:

That is becoming for a courtly knight who keeps the rules."

"Sweet one, unsay that speech," said the brave man,

"For I dared not do that lest I be denied.

If I were forward and were refused, the fault would be mine."

"But none," said the noblewoman, "could deny you, by my faith!

You are strong enough to constrain with your strength if you wish,

If any were so ill-bred as to offer you resistance."

"Yes, good guidance you give me, by God," replied Gawain,

"But threateners are ill thought of and do not thrive in my country,

Nor do gifts thrive when given without good will.

I am here at your behest, to offer a kiss to when you like;

You may do it whenever you deem fit, or desist,

  In this place."

  The beautiful lady bent

  And fairly kissed his face;

  Much speech the two then spent

  On love, its grief and grace.

甚至当我挑明了仍置之不理!
昨天我以十分明确的方式关照你,
想不到今天你已忘得一干二净。"
"你指的是什么?"骑士疑惑地问,"我确实不知,
如果我装聋作哑,那真该受谴责。"
"我指的是亲吻,"美人儿说,
"当恩惠施与人,这恩惠必须马上接受,
这是规矩,适合高贵的骑士遵守。"
"好人儿,请别这么说,"勇敢的骑士说,
"我不敢这样做,是因为害怕被拒绝,
如果我自讨没趣,那就是我的过错。"
"我担保,"贵妇人说,"没有人会拒绝你,
即使缺乏教养的人会不依从,
你也有足够的毅力克制自己。"
"上帝做证,你使我茅塞顿开,"高文回答,
"但在我的家乡,恐吓别人要遭唾弃,
送人礼物不出于善意也不讨人欢喜。
我在此听从你的吩咐,随时可以吻你,
眼下你如果觉得合适,也可以

       让你满意。"

    漂亮的夫人弯下身,
    热烈地亲吻了他的脸,
    两人促膝长谈爱情,
    包括它的甜美与辛酸。

60

"I WOULD know of you, knight," the noble lady said.

"If it did not anger you, what argument you use,

Being so hale and hearty as you are at this time,

So generous a gentleman as you are justly famed to be;

Since the choicest thing in Chivalry, the chief thing praised,

Is the loyal sport of love, the very lore of arms?

For the tale of the contentions of true knights

Is told by the title and text of their feats,

How lords for their true loves put their lives at hazard,

Endured dreadful trials for their dear loves' sakes,

And with valour avenged and made void their woes,

Bringing home abundant bliss by their virtues.

You are the gentlest and most just of your generation;

Everywhere your honour and high fame are known;

Yet I have sat at your side two separate times here

Without hearing you utter in any way

A single syllable of the saga of love.

Being so polished and punctilious a pledge-fulfiller,

You ought to be eager to lay open to a young thing

Your discoveries in the craft of courtly love.

What! Are you ignorant, with all your renown?

60

"骑士,如果你不生气,"高贵的夫人说,
"我想知道你如何看待爱情:
你眼下是如此生气勃勃的一个人,
如此闻名而慷慨的一位绅士,
我问你,骑士之道中最被称道的东西
是否就是忠诚的爱情,那追风求凰的学问?
说到真正骑士的丰功伟绩,
有关的铭文和传说都这样记载:
他们为了真正的爱情将生死置之度外,
为了自己的心上人忍受可怕的考验,
最后勇敢地报了仇,摆脱了悲伤,
欢天喜地返回自己的家园。
你是这类人中最温良正直的一个;
你的荣誉和令名早已播布四方;
但我单独坐在你身边已是第二回,
却始终没有听你说起
有关你的爱情故事的只言片语。
既然你如此高雅而讲究信用,
就应该向一个美人吐露胸怀,
跟她说说你在情场上的所见所闻。
怎么?你这样的名人居然会无此经历?

Or do you deem me too dull to drink in your dalliance?

    For shame!

      I sit here unchaperoned, and stay

      To acquire some courtly game;

      So while my lord is away,

      Teach me your true wit's fame."

61

"IN good faith," said Gawain, "may God requite you!

It gives me great happiness, and is good sport to me,

That so fine a fair one as you should find her way here

And take pains with so poor a man, make pastime with her knight,

With any kind of clemency—it comforts me greatly.

But for me to take on the travail of interpreting true love

And construing the subjects of the stories of arms

To you who, I hold, have more skill

In that art, by half, than a hundred of such

As I am or ever shall be on the earth I inhabit,

Would in faith be a manifold folly, noble lady.

To please you I would press with all the power in my soul,

For I am highly beholden to you, and evermore shall be

True servant to your bounteous self, so save me God!"

So that stately lady tempted him and tried him with questions

你是否觉得我太愚钝,不配领略个中风情?

　　真难为情呀!

　　我在这里无人监视,

　　意欲得到高雅享受;

　　我的丈夫正好外出,

　　请你教我如何情游。"

61

"愿上帝保佑你,"高文说,

"我感到非常幸福,我玩得极其开心,

有你这样一位美人在这里

耐着性子与我这可怜的骑士消遣,

你的美意让我感到无比欣慰。

但是,要让我费神谈论爱情,

叙述温柔的风流韵事给你听,

高贵的夫人,那真是荒谬透顶,

因为你自己就是情场里手

像我这样的人一百个也比不上你,

无论现在或将来,我永远望尘莫及。

为了让你高兴,我如今只有尽力而为,

我受你的恩惠太多,作为报答,

我会永远做你的奴仆,愿上帝助我!"

就这样,高贵的夫人千方百计引诱他,

To win him to wickedness, whatever else she thought.

But he defended himself so firmly that no fault appeared,

Nor was there any evil apparent on either side,

But bliss;

For long they laughed and played

Till she gave him a gracious kiss.

A fond farewell she bade,

And went her way on this.

62

SIR Gawain bestirred himself and went to mass:

Then dinner was dressed and with due honour served.

All day long the lord and the ladies disported,

But the castellan coursed across the country time and again,

Hunted his hapless boar as it hurtled over the hills,

Then bit the backs of his best hounds asunder

Standing at bay, till the bowmen obliged him to break free

Out into the open for all he could do,

So fast the arrows flew when the folk there concentrated.

Even the strongest he sometimes made start back,

But in time he became so tired he could tear away no more,

And with the speed he still possessed, he spurted to a hole

On a rise by a rock with a running stream beside.

用种种试探想导致他犯罪，

但高文严加戒备，始终不动妄念，

因此，两人间除了谈笑没有发生

任何丑事。

两人说笑许久时间，

最后她给他热烈一吻。

起身向他说声再见，

然后独自出了房门。

62

高文振奋精神去做弥撒，

然后在午宴上备受款待。

一整天男男女女嬉戏行乐，

而城堡主则又奔驰在郊外，

追捕那头横冲直撞的倒霉野猪。

最好的猎犬被它咬伤背部，

但猎手们仍将它驱赶得走投无路，

只得突出重围奔向一片开阔地；

猎手在那里聚齐后又纷纷向它射箭，

野猪一次次逼得最勇敢的人也不敢上前，

但它终于累得不能再撕咬了，

不过，它仍善于奔跑，并冲进一个山洞，

那地方就在斜坡的岩石旁，紧挨一条小溪。

He got the bank at his back, and began to abrade the ground.

The froth was foaming foully at his mouth,

And he whetted his white tusks; a weary time it was

For the bold men about, who were bound to harass him

From a distance, for none dared to draw near him

      For dread.

    He has hurt so many men

    That is entered no one's head

    To be torn by his tusks again,

    And he raging and seeing red.

63

TILL the castellan came himself, encouraging his horse,

And saw the boar at bay with his band of men around.

He alighted in lively fashion, left his courser,

Drew and brandished his bright sword and boldly strode forward,

Striding at speed through the stream to where the savage beast was.

The wild thing was aware of the weapon and its wielder,

And so bridled with its bristles in a burst of fierce snorts

That all were anxious for the lord, lest he have the worst of it.

Straight away the savage brute sprang at the man,

And baron and boar were both in a heap

In the swirling water: the worst went to the beast,

野猪用背抵住堤岸,擦着躯体,
污秽的白沫顺着嘴角淌下,
一边还磨砺着那一对白森森的獠牙,
猎手们已十分疲惫,只能远远攻击它,
由于心怀畏惧,没有人敢靠近
　　这头野猪。
　　它已经伤了许多射手,
　　没有人还有那份胆量,
　　让这两眼发红的猛兽,
　　再次用长牙将他拱翻。

63

直到城堡主自己催马过来,
看见穷途末路的野猪与猎手在相持,
他便敏捷地翻身下鞍,离开他的坐骑,
抽出闪亮的宝剑,挥舞着大步上前,
迅速穿过溪流,来到猛兽的藏身地。
那畜生一看见那武器和来人,
便鬃毛倒竖,发出一阵可怕的哼哼声,
大伙都为主人担忧,唯恐他大难临头。
凶猛的野猪即刻扑向勋爵,
人和兽同时踏进湍流,
大难临头的是那头野兽,

For the man had marked him well at the moment of impact,

Had put the point precisely at the pit of his chest,

And drove it in to the hilt, so that the heart was shattered,

And the spent beast sank snarling and was swept downstream,

Teeth bare,

A hundred hounds and more

Attack and seize and tear;

Men tug him to the shore

And the dogs destroy him there.

64

BUGLES blew the triumph, horns blared loud.

There was hallooing in high pride by all present;

Braches bayed at the beast, as bidden by their masters,

The chief huntsmen in charge of that chase so hard.

Then one who was wise in wood-crafts

Started in style to slash open the boar.

First he hewed off the head and hoisted it on high,

Then rent him roughly along the ridge of his back,

Brought out the bowels and broiled them on coals

For blending with bread as the braches' reward.

Then he broke out the brawn from the bright broad flanks,

Took out the offal, as is fit,

因为就在人兽相撞的一刹那，
骑士及时出剑，正好刺中野猪的胸口，
这一剑深至剑柄，穿透了野猪的心脏，
垂死的野兽哼叫着跌进水里，它的钢牙
　　依然裸露。
　　无数猎犬蜂拥而上，
　　对野猪又咬又抓又撕，
　　猎手们把它拖上岸，
　　猎犬继续摧残那兽尸。

64

胜利的号角吹得震天响，
所有人自豪地欢呼喝彩；
参加这次艰难围猎的众猎手嗾使猎犬，
让它们对着猎物齐声吠叫。
一位熟谙行猎之道的老猎手
开始用屠刀解剖这头野兽。
他先剁下它的头，把它高高挂起，
然后沿着背脊艰难地剖开肚子，
掏出里面的肠子，放在炭火上熏过
然后掺进面包作为猎犬的奖赏。
他接着切开宽厚的腰窝，
有条不紊地取出里面的内脏，

Attached the two halves entirely together,

And on a strong stake stoutly hung them.

Then home they hurried with the huge beast,

With the boar's head borne before the baron himself,

Who had destroyed him in the stream by the strength of his arm,

Above all:

It seemed to him an age

Till he greeted Gawain in hall.

To reap his rightful wage

The latter came at his call.

65

THE lord exclaimed loudly, laughing merrily

When he saw Sir Gawain, and spoke joyously.

The sweet ladies were sent for, and the servants assembled.

Then he showed them the shields, and surely described

The large size and length, and the malignity

Of the fierce boar's fighting when he fled in the woods;

So that Gawain congratulated him on his great deed,

Commended it as a merit he had mainfested well,

For a beast with so much brawn, the bold man said,

A boar of such breadth, he had not before seen.

When they handled the huge head the upright man praised it,

然后把剖开的两半重新合拢，

把它们绑到一根坚硬的杠子上。

他们抬着巨兽急急回家，

那个猪头就归勋爵所有，

因为是他凭非凡的勇力在溪边杀死

这头猛兽。

这城堡主迫不及待，

很想马上见到高文；

骑士应召随即赶来，

领取他应得的"酬金"。

65

城堡主见到高文十分高兴，

他扯开嗓门说话，笑得好不开心！

太太们都来了，仆人们也围拢过来。

城堡主给大家看厚厚的猪皮，

详尽地描述猎物的大小和长度，

追述如何在林中与逃窜的野猪殊死相搏，

高文对他的壮举表示祝贺，

称赞它是一件天日昭然的伟绩，

因为如此强壮的野猪，高文说，

他有生以来还是第一次见识。

当人们抬过猪头，城堡主赞不绝口，

Expressed horror thereat for the ear of the lord.

"Now Gawain," said the good man, "this game is your own

By our contracted treaty, in truth, you know,"

"It is so," said the knight, "and as certainly

I shall give you all my gains as guerdon, in faith."

He clasped the castellan's neck and kissed him kindly,

And then served him a second time in the same style.

"In all our transactions since I came to sojourn," asserted Gawain,

"Up to tonight, as of now, there's nothing that

      I owe."

     "By Saint Giles," the castellan quipped,

     "You're the finest fellow I know:

     Your wealth will have us whipped

     If your trade continues so!"

66

THEN the trestles and tables were trimly set out,

Complete with cloths, and clearly flaming cressets

And waxen torches were placed in the wall-brackets

By retainers, who then tended the entire hall-gathering.

Much gladness and glee then gushed forth there

By the fire on the floor: and in multifarious ways

They sang noble songs at supper and afterwards,

诉说那野兽的吼叫声如何吓人。

"高文,"善良的人说,"根据我们的契约,

这头野猪已完全归你所有。"

"正是如此,"骑士回答,"但作为回报,

我也要把我的收获如数交出。"

他说完抱住城堡主给他热烈一吻,

紧接着如法炮制又添了一个。

"自从我在此逗留,"高文保证,

"到目前为止,我在这场交易中没有

　　　　　拖欠分文。"

　　"圣吉尔斯做证,"城堡主戏语,

　　你真是个难得的好人,

　　你的财富将超过我们,

　　只要保持如此的收成。"[20]

66

然后桌子摆设整齐,铺上台布,

支架上摆着火光清幽的灯盏,

仆人们在临墙的托架上插上蜡烛,

忙着照料济济一堂的宾客。

灯火通明的大厅一片欢腾,

晚餐前后,他们还用各式的音调,

唱起一支支高雅的歌,

A concert of Christmas carols and new dance songs,

With the most mannerly mirth a man could tell of,

And our courteous knight kept constant company with the lady.

In a bewitchingly well-mannered way she made up to him,

Secretly soliciting the stalwart knight

So that he was astounded, and upset in himself.

But his upbringing forbade him to rebuff her utterly,

So he behaved towards her honourably, whatever aspersions might

Be cast.

They revelled in the hall

As long as their pleasure might last

And then at the castellan's call

To the chamber hearth they passed.

67

THERE they drank and discoursed and decided to enjoy

Similar solace and sport on New Year's Eve.

But the princely knight asked permission to depart in the morning,

For his appointed time was approaching, and perforce he must go.

But the lord would not let him and implored him to linger,

Saying, "I swear to you, as a staunch true knight,

You shall gain the Green Chapel to give your dues,

My lord, in the light of New Year, long before sunrise.

圣诞颂歌伴和着新谱的舞曲，
欢乐的气氛难以用语言描述。
我们谦恭的骑士一直陪伴着夫人。
她以令人销魂的姿态靠近他，
并向这位强健的骑士悄悄恳求，
这使他大为震惊，心慌意乱。
但良好的教养提醒他切莫上当，
不管别人如何诽谤，他对她始终
　　　礼貌有加。
　　他们狂欢在大厅，
　　尽情享乐度时光，
　　直到城堡主传令，
　　才各自返回卧房。

67

新年前夕，他们饮酒，谈天，
继续欢欢喜喜把时光消磨。
但高贵的骑士一早要求离开，
因为期限已近，他必须上路。
城堡主不让他走，执意要挽留，
他说："我以骑士的信誉向你担保，
我的爵爷，新年这天，太阳升起以前，
你定能找到绿色教堂完成你的使命。

Therefore remain in your room and rest in comfort,

While I fare hunting in the forest; in fulfilment of our oath

Exchanging what we achieve when the chase is over.

For twice I have tested you, and twice found you true.

Now 'Third time, throw best!' Think of that tomorrow!

Let us make merry while we may, set our minds on joy,

For hard fate can hit man whenever it likes."

This was graciously granted and Gawain stayed.

Blithely drink was brought, then to bed with lights

      They pressed.

   All night Sir Gawain sleeps

   Softly and still at rest;

   But the lord his custom keeps

   And is early up and dressed.

68

AFTER mass, he and his men made a small meal.

Merry was the morning; he demanded his horse.

The men were ready mounted before the main gate,

A host of knightly horsemen to follow after him.

Wonderfully fair was the forest-land, for the frost remained,

And the rising sun shone ruddily on the ragged clouds,

In its beauty brushing their blackness off the heavens.

在我林中打猎期间,你尽管待在房里,

舒舒服服休息,等我打猎归来

再履行诺言交换我们的收获。

我已考验你两回,发现你每回都忠诚。

这第三回最关键! 请你想想自己的明天!

让我们玩个尽兴,一心只图快活,

因为残酷的命运随时会降临。"

高文爽快地答应他继续留下。

两人开始畅饮,直到睡意袭来,不得不

举灯入房。

高文爵士心情平静

舒舒服服睡到天亮;

城堡主则一如先前,

早早起来穿衣着装。

68

弥撒以后,他和他的扈从草草用过早餐,

清晨一片欢乐;他吩咐为他备马。

大伙在大门口整装待发,

一大班勇敢的骑士追随在他左右。

林间美不胜收,严霜覆木依旧,

火红的太阳从破碎的云层升起,

壮丽中将黑暗驱逐出天际。

The huntsmen unleashed the hounds by a holt-side,

And the rocks and surrounding bushes rang with their horn-calls.

Some found and followed the fox's tracks,

And wove various ways in their wily fashion.

A small hound cried the scent, the senior huntsman called

His fellow foxhounds to him and, feverishly sniffing,

The rout of dogs rushed forward on the right path.

The fox hurried fast, for they found him soon

And, seeing him distinctly, pursued him at speed,

Unmistakably giving tongue with tumultuous din.

Deviously in difficult country he doubled on his tracks,

Swerved and wheeled away, often waited listening,

Till at last by a little ditch he leaped a quickset hedge,

And stole out stealthily at the side of a valley,

Considering his stratagem had given the slip to the hounds.

But he stumbled on a tracking-dogs' tryst-place unawares,

And there in a cleft three hounds threatened him at once,

>   All grey.

> He swiftly started back,

> And, full of deep dismay,

> He dashed on a different track;

> To the woods he went away.

猎手们在丛林边放出猎犬，
山崖和灌木丛回荡着阵阵号角声。
猎手中有人发现了狐狸的足迹，
他们用尽心机布下捕捉的罗网。
一只小猎犬闻到了气味，年长的猎手
呼唤他的猎狐犬仔细嗅探，
成群的猎犬沿着正确的路径呼啸而上。
狐狸急急逃窜，因为人们已发现它，
并且看得一清二楚，大伙于是全速追击，
山谷里传来他们嘈杂的吆喝。
狡猾的狐狸在茂密的林地左冲右突，
东折西转，不时地停下聆听，
直到在小溪边跳过一丛山楂，
悄悄地沿着山谷溜出包围圈。
它以为这一招已把猎犬骗过，
谁知不知不觉又闯入它们的营地。
山口里即刻蹿出三只灰犬威胁着
　　　　它的性命。
　　狐狸急忙返身逃跑，
　　慌慌张张满腹酸辛，
　　它窜上另一条小道，
　　急急钻进茂密丛林。

165

69

THEN came the lively delight of listening to hounds
When they had all met in a muster, mingling together,
For, catching sight of him, they cried such curses on him
That the clustering cliffs seemed to be crashing down.
Here he was hallooed when the hunters met him,
There savagely snarled at by intercepting hounds;
Then he was called thief and threatened often;
With the tracking dogs on his tail, no tarrying was possible.
When out in the open he was often run at,
So he often swerved in again, that artful Reynard.
Yes, he led the lord and his liegemen a dance
In this manner among the mountains till mid-afternoon,
While harmoniously at home the honoured knight slept
Between the comely curtains in the cold morning.
But the lady's longing to woo would not let her sleep,
Nor would she impair the purpose pitched in her heart,
But rose up rapidly and ran to him
In a ravishing robe that reached to the ground,
Trimmed with finest fur from pure pelts;
Not coifed as to custom, but with costly jewels

69

猎犬闻声而动，一只只欢欣雀跃，
它们很快聚集到一起，因为
它们已看见它，高声向它吠叫，
那声音简直要将林立的山崖震倒。
这边，有猎手对着它大声吆喝，
那边，有阻截的猎犬猖猖咆哮。
猎手们不断叫它"小偷"，发出威胁的喊声。
猎犬在背后追，它一刻也不能停留。
一旦进入开阔地，猎犬便穷追不舍，
狡猾的列那[21]只好突然转变方向。
就这样，它领着城堡主及其众猎手
在丛林中一直周旋到午后很久。
而此时城堡里那位可敬的骑士
却已舒舒服服躺在罗帐里一上午。
追切求爱的夫人使他不得安睡，
她早已打定主意，不肯轻易罢休，
急急起床后就跑到他身边，
令人销魂的长袍拖曳在地，
饰边的皮毛纯净而漂亮。
无数的珠子缀满了她的发网，

Strung in scores on her splendid hairnet.
Her fine-featured face and fair throat were unveiled,
Her breast was bare and her back as well.
She came in by the chamber door and closed it after her,
Cast open a casement and called on the knight,
And briskly thus rebuked him with bountiful words

  Of good cheer.
   "Ah sir! What, sound asleep?
   The morning's crisp and clear."
   He had been drowsing deep,
   But now he had to hear.

     70

THE noble sighed ceaselessly in unsettled slumber
As threatening thoughts thronged in the dawn light
About destiny, which the day after would deal him his fate
At the Green Chapel where Gawain was to greet his man,
And be bound to bear his buffet unresisting.
But having recovered consciousness in comely fashion,
He heaved himself out of dreams and answered hurriedly.
The lovely lady advanced, laughing adorably,
Swooped over his splendid face and sweetly kissed him.
He welcomed her worthily with noble cheer

如此的装扮并非风俗使然。
白嫩的脸蛋和脖子毫无遮蔽，
赫然裸露的还有胸口和背脊。
她走进卧室，随手把门关上，
打开一扇窗，过来招呼骑士，
一开口便眉飞色舞，用戏言

　　　　斥责高文。

　　"爵士，晚上睡得香不香？
早上的空气真够清新！"
他懵懵懂懂刚离开梦乡，
只好打起精神来恭听。

70

骑士心慌意乱，长吁短叹，
一大早他思虑的是险恶的命运，
第二天他就得经受生死考验，
去绿色教堂会见那个怪人，
毫无抵抗地接受他的打击。
但他很快镇静地回过神来，
不再胡思乱想，迅速做出反应。
可爱的夫人笑盈盈地走到他跟前
凑上俊俏的脸给他甜甜的一吻。
他彬彬有礼向她表示欢迎，

And, gazing on her gay and glorious attire,
Her features so faultless and fine of complexion,
He felt a flush of rapture suffuse his heart.
Sweet and genial smiling slid them into joy
Till bliss burst forth between them, beaming gay
      And bright;
    With joy the two contended
    In talk of true delight,
    And peril would have impended
    Had Mary not minded her knight.

71

FOR that peerless princess pressed him so hotly,
So invited him to the very verge, that he felt forced
Either to allow her love or blackguardly rebuff her.
He was concerned for his courtesy, lest he be called caitiff,
But more especially for his evil plight if he should plunge into sin,
And dishonour the owner of the house treacherously.
"God shield me! That shall not happen, for sure," said the knight.
So with laughing love-talk he deflected gently
The downright declarations that dropped from her lips.
Said the beauty to the bold man, "Blame will be yours
If you love not the living body lying close to you

两眼注视着那一身艳丽的衣装,

她的容貌无疵无瑕,光彩四射,

他感到一阵心跳,神魂颠倒。

甜美而温柔的微笑悄悄流露,

直到双方春风满面,极大的喜悦

　　　　　溢于言表。

　　　在乐融融的交谈中,

　　　两人的兴致都很高,

　　　危险已经悬在半空,

　　　如果没有圣母关照。

71

美貌绝伦的夫人感情那么热烈,

使高文差点做出两种选择:

要么接受她的爱,要么严词拒绝。

但他更重视礼义,唯恐被人称为卑鄙之陡,

更懂得放纵自己意味着犯罪,

背叛了城堡的主人,给他脸上抹黑。

"请主保护! 此事绝不能发生,"骑士说。

他于是把她亲口说出的许诺

在说说笑笑的情谈中悄悄回避。

美人儿对骑士说:"你真该受谴责!

一位伤心的女子就躺在你身边,

More than all wooers in the world who are wounded in heart;

Unless you have a lover more beloved, who delights you more,

A maiden to whom you are committed, so immutably bound

That you do not seek to sever from her—which I see is so.

Tell me the truth of it, I entreat you now;

By all the loves there are, do not hide the truth

    With guile."

      Then gently, "By Saint John,"

      Said the knight with a smile,

      "I owe my oath to none,

      Nor wish to yet a while."

72

"THOSE words," said the fair woman, "are the worst there could be,

But I am truly answered, to my utter anguish.

Give me now a gracious kiss, and I shall go from here

As a maid that loves much, mourning on this earth."

Then, sighing, she stooped, and seemlily kissed him,

And, severing herself from him, stood up and said,

"At this adieu, my dear one, do me this pleasure:

Give me something as gift, your glove if no more,

To mitigate my mourning when I remember you."

"Now certainly, for your sake," said the knight,

你却无动于衷,视同一般的求婚者。
你是否已有更称心的心上人?
是否已跟某位姑娘山盟海誓,
永远不跟她分离?我看原因就在这里。
我恳求你把实情说给我听听,
看在我一片痴情的分上,请如实相告,
　　　别耍花招。"

　　骑士笑了笑,轻声说:
　　"让圣约翰为我做证,
　　我从没有立过誓约,
　　也不希望此事发生。"

72

　　"你的话,"美妇人说,"实在糟糕透顶,
但我已得到回答,尽管它令人伤心。
慷慨地给我一个吻吧,我这就走,
就像一名多情的少女哀悼人间的薄情。"
她叹息着弯下腰,优雅地给他一吻
然后站起身,准备离去,这时她又说:
　　"亲爱的,在这离别之际,我有一事相求:
请给我一件礼物,你的手套也行,
好让我想念你时痛苦有所减轻。"
　　"为了你这当然应该,"骑士说,

'I wish I had here the handsomest thing I own,

For you have deserved, forsooth, superabundantly

And rightfully, a richer reward than I could give.

But as tokens of true love, trifles mean little.

It is not to your honour to have at this time

A mere glove as Gawain's gift to treasure.

For I am here on an errand in unknown regious,

And have no bondsmen, no baggages with dear-bought things in them.

This afflicts me now, fair lady, for your sake.

Man must do as he must; neither lament it

      Nor repine."

    "No, highly honoured one,"

    Replied that lady fine,

    "Though gift you give me none,

    You must have something of mine."

73

SHE proffered him a rich ring wrought in red gold,

With a sparkling stone set conspicuously in it,

Which beamed as brilliantly as the bright sun;

You may well believe its worth was wonderfully great.

But the courteous man declined it and quickly said,

"Before God, gracious lady, no giving just now!

"我希望身边有最美妙的礼物，

因为你确实有理由得到

比我现在能给的更好的馈赠。

作为爱情的见证，礼轻意味情轻。

高文的礼物如只是一只手套，

这与你的荣誉实在不相称。

但可惜我此次出游有事在身，

既没带仆人，也没带贵重的物品。

为此我感到十分难过，美丽的夫人。

男子汉应敢作敢为，我的命运既不必哀悼，

　　　也不必怨怼。"

　　"不错，高贵的骑士，"

　　美丽的夫人回答他，

　　"既然你无物相遗，

　　我的心意仍需表达。"

73

她呈上一枚金红色的戒指，

上面镶嵌着硕大的宝石，

它光芒四射犹如明亮的金乌。

你可以相信，这戒指价值连城。

但彬彬有礼的骑士赶紧婉言拒绝，

"上帝做证，慷慨的夫人，别把它给我，

Not having anything to offer, I shall accept nothing."

She offered it him urgently and he refused again,

Fast affirming his refusal on his faith as a knight.

Put out by this repulse, she presently said,

"If you reject my ring as too rich in value,

Doubtless you would be less deeply indebted to me

If I gave you my girdle, a less gainful gift."

She swiftly slipped off the cincture of her gown

Which went round her waist under the wonderful mantle,

A girdle of green silk with a golden hem,

Embroidered only at the edges, with hand-stitched ornament.

And she pleaded with the prince in a pleasant manner

To take it notwithstanding its trifling worth;

But he told her that he could touch no treasure at all,

Not gold nor any gift, till God gave him grace

To pursue to success the search he was bound on.

"And therefore I beg you not to be displeased:

Press no more your purpose, for I promise it never

  Can be.

  I owe you a hundredfold

  For grace you have granted me;

  And ever through hot and cold

  I shall stay your devotee."

别送我任何礼物,我什么也不要。"

她急切要给,他一再推托,

并以骑士的信誉作为借口。

他的拒绝刺痛了她的心,她说:

"如果你觉得拒绝戒指是因为它太贵重,

那我就给你一根腰带,它价值不大,

你一定不会觉得对我负债累累。"

她迅速从长袍上摘下一根腰带,

它原先系在腰间,被外衣遮掩。

这是一根绿色绸带,镶有金边,

那装饰物全用手工缝制。

夫人态度诚恳,要求骑士收下,

尽管它的价值并不太大。

但他告诉她,他不能接受任何馈赠,

无论金子还是别的礼物,

直到上帝慈悲,让他在探险中凯旋。

"因此我恳求你不要难过,

别再逼我,因为我敢保证,此事

　　　确实不妥。

　　由于你待人慷慨大方,

　　我欠你的情水长山高,

　　从今后无论火海刀山,

　　我都甘愿为夫人效劳。"

74

"Do you say 'no' to this silk?" then said the beauty,
"Because it is simple in itself? And so it seems.
Lo! It is little indeed, and so less worth your esteem.
But one who was aware of the worth twined in it
Would appraise its properties as more precious perhaps,
For the man that binds his body with this belt of green,
As long as he laps it closely about him,
No hero under heaven can hack him to pieces,
For he cannot be killed by any cunninng on earth."
Then the prince pondered, and it appeared to him
A precious gem to protect him in the peril appointed him
When he gained the Green Chapel to be given checkmate:
It would be a splendid stratagem to escape being slain.
Then he allowed her to solicit him and let her speak.
She pressed the belt upon him with potent words
And having got his agreement, she gave it him gladly,
Beseeching him for her sake to conceal it always,
And hide it from her husband with all diligence.
That never should another know of it, the noble swore
      Outright.
    Then often his thanks gave he

74

"这腰带你也拒绝？"美人儿问，
"是不是因为它太不值钱？不错，
它确实很不显眼，难怪你小看它。
但只要你知道它的真正价值，
也许就会对它另眼看待。
谁愿意把这绿腰带系在身上，
只要它紧紧贴着他的身体，
世上任何英雄都砍他不死，
因为它能让佩带者刀枪不入。"
骑士陷入沉思：它能在危难时提供保护，
这宝贝对他来说倒也珍贵，
因为他得前往绿色教堂接受斧砍，
这腰带正好充当逃生的法宝。
他于是任凭她谆谆劝诱；
她则不失时机一个劲催促，
得到同意后，她高兴地递过腰带，
并关照他为了她把此事永远隐瞒，
千万别让她的丈夫得知内情。
高贵的骑士即刻发誓，他决不让别人
　　　　知道此事。
　　然后高文诚心诚意

With all his heart and might,
And thrice by then had she
Kissed the constant knight.

75

THEN with a word of farewell she went away,
For she could not force further satisfaction from him.
Directly she withdrew, Sir Gawain dressed himself,
Rose and arrayed himself in rich garments,
But laid aside the love-lace the lady had given him,
Secreted it carefully where he could discover it later.
Then he went his way at once to the chapel,
Privily approached a priest and prayed him there
To listen to his life's sins and enlighten him
On how he might have salvation in the hereafter.
Then, confessing his faults, he fairly shrove himself,
Begging mercy for both major and minor sins.
He asked the holy man for absolution
And was absolved with certainty and sent out so pure
That Doomsday could have been declared the day after.
Then he made merrier among the noble ladies,
With comely carolling and all kinds of pleasure,
Than ever he had done, with ecstasy, till came

再次向她表示谢忱，
她随即一口气给了
忠诚的骑士三个吻。

75

她最后向他告辞，走出卧房，
因为她无法强迫他给她更多的满足。
夫人一走，高文爵士赶紧穿衣起床，
披上他那件华丽的外氅。
他把夫人送的腰带小心藏起，
以便以后再把它悄悄带走。
这以后他便即刻上路去教堂，
将一位神甫秘密拜访，
向神甫忏悔，让他听听他犯下的罪过，
开导他如何拯救自己的灵魂。
他承认自己的过失，并祈求赦罪，
祈求对他的种种罪孽大发慈悲。
他向那位教职人员忏悔自己，
得到明确的赦免后出了教堂，
即使明天就是末日审判，于他也已无妨。
他于是高高兴兴与贵妇们待在一起，
唱唱欢乐的歌曲，玩玩各种游戏，
比以往过得更惬意，直到

Dark night.

Such honour he did to all,

They said, "Never has this knight

Since coming into hall

Expressed such pure delight."

76

NOW long may he linger there, love sheltering him!

The prince was still on the plain, pleasuring in the chase,

Having finished off the fox he had followed so far.

As he leaped over a hedge looking out for the quarry,

Where he heard the hounds that were harrying the fox,

Reynard came running through a rough thicket

With the pack all pell-mell, panting at his heels.

The lord, aware of the wild beast, waited craftily,

Then drew his dazzling sword and drove at the fox.

The beast baulked at the blade to break sideways,

But a dog bounded at him before he could,

And right in front of the horse's feet they fell on him,

All worrying their wily prey with a wild uproar.

The lord quickly alighted and lifted him up,

Wrenched him beyond reach of the ravening fangs,

Held him high over his head and hallooed lustily,

夜幕降临。

他给大家带来荣耀，
人们说："自从这位骑士
来到我们这座城堡，
第一次见他如此欢喜。"

76

但愿高文长此以往，永受爱情庇护！
城堡主仍在丛林追赶那只狐狸，
终于把它杀死，获得行猎的欢喜。
当时他骑马跃过树篱寻找猎物，
只听见猎犬正朝着狐狸狂吠，
列那从茂密的灌木丛中蹿出，
一大群猎犬在背后紧紧追击。
深知野兽习性的城堡主看准时机，
抽出闪光的宝剑刺向那只狐狸。
列那在刀刃前突然止步，蹿向一侧，
但猎犬没等它逃开就把它扑住，
它们在马蹄前展开围攻，
大声吠叫着啮咬狡猾的野兽。
城堡主赶紧下马把狐狸提在手里，
猛烈扭动它，不让猎犬继续撕咬。
他把它举过头顶，大声欢呼，

While the angry hounds in hordes bayed at him.

Thither hurried the huntsmen with horns in plenty,

Sounding the rally splendidly till they saw their lord.

When the company of his court had come up to the kill,

All who bore bugles blew at once,

And the others without horns hallooed loudly.

The requiem that was raised for Reynard's soul

And the commotion made it the merriest meet ever,

> Men said.

> The hounds must have their fee:

> They pat them on the head,

> Then hold the fox; and he

> Is reft of his skin of red.

77

THEN they set off for home, it being almost night,

Blowing their big horns bravely as they went.

At last the lord alighted at his beloved castle

And found upon the floor a fire, and beside it

The good Sir Gawain in a glad humour

By reason of the rich friendship he had reaped from the ladies.

He wore a turquoise tunic extending to the ground;

His softly-furred surcoat suited him well,

愤怒的猎犬围着他狂吠乱叫。

猎手们带着号角急急赶来，

集结号声吹起，他们来到主子身边。

城堡主的扈从一看见猎物，

带号角的便吹响了号角，

没带号角的则高声呼喊。

安灵曲开始为列那的灵魂颂唱，

大伙都说，那乱哄哄的场面

其乐无穷。

猎犬必须得到奖励，

他们拍拍它们的头；

然后拖过那只狐狸，

剥下它火红的毛皮，

77

时近黄昏，他们出发回家，

一路上吹响嘹亮的喇叭。

城堡主终于在可爱的城堡前下马，

发现大厅里已燃起炉火，

高文爵士就待在炉膛边，

沉浸在女士们的友谊中，显得神采奕奕。

他身穿一件宽大的束腰外衣，

皮毛柔软的上装十分适合他的身段。

And his hood of the same hue hung from his shoulder.

All trimmed with ermine were hood and surcoat.

Meeting the master in the middle of the floor,

Gawain went forward gladly and greeted him thus:

"Forthwith, I shall be the first to fulfil the contract

We settled so suitably without sparing the wine."

Then he clasped the castellan and kissed him thrice

As sweetly and steadily as a strong knight could.

"By Christ!' quoth the other, 'You will carve yourself a fortune

By traffic in this trade when the terms suit you!'

"Do not chop logic about the exchange," chipped in Gawain,

"As I have properly paid over the profit I made."

"Marry," said the other man, "Mine is inferior,

For I have hunted all day and have only taken

This ill-favoured fox's skin, may the Fiend take it!

And that is a poor price to pay for such precious things

As you have pressed upon me here, three pure kisses

      So good."

    "Enough!" acknowledged Gawain,

    "I thank you, by the Rood."

    And how the fox was slain

    The lord told him as they stood.

同色兜帽从他的肩上垂下，
上装和兜帽都饰有貂皮。
他在大厅正中迎接城堡主，
高兴地走上前跟他招呼：
"这次我要提前履行契约，
不像先前边饮酒边交换礼物。"
说完他抱住城堡主，按骑士的礼节
亲切而热烈地吻了他三次。
"基督做证，"城堡主说，"这场买卖，
你鸿运高照，将大发横财！"
"别把话说颠倒，"高文戏言，
"我只是负债人偿还欠债。"
"哎呀，"城堡主说，"我的礼物太轻，
因为我围猎了一整天，只得到
这张丑陋的狐皮，真是倒霉透顶！
刚才你给了我三个纯洁的吻，
如此珍贵的东西我无以奉还，只有这
　　　区区薄礼。"
　　"这足够了！"高文回答他，
　　"十字架做证，我感谢你。"
　　狐狸如何被猎手捕杀，
　　城堡主说得详详细细。

78

WITH mirth and minstrelsy, and meals when they liked,

They made as merry then as ever men could;

With the laughter of ladies and delightful jesting,

Gawain and his good host were very gay together,

Save when excess or sottishness seemed likely.

Master and men made many a witty sally,

Until presently, at the appointed parting-time,

The brave men were bidden to bed at last.

Then of his host the hero humbly took leave,

The first to bid farewell, fairly thanking him:

"May the High King requite you for your courtesy at this feast,

And the wonderful week of my dwelling here!

I would offer to be one of your own men if you liked,

But that I must move on tomorrow, as you know,

If you will give me the guide you granted me,

To show me the Green Chapel where my share of doom

Will be dealt on New Year's Day, as God deems for me."

"With all my heart!" said the host. "In good faith,

All that I ever promised you, I shall perform."

He assigned him a servant to set him on his way,

And lead him in the hills without any delay,

78

他们在欢歌声中共进晚餐，

人世间再没有人比他们更快活。

在夫人小姐的欢声笑语中，

高文和城堡主欢欢喜喜待在一起，

那情景真好像醉人的狂欢，

主人和他的臣属妙语连珠，

说说笑笑一直闹腾到分手，

勇士们终于按吩咐上床就寝。

我们的英雄谦恭地向主人告辞，

特意向他表示由衷的谢忱：

"愿天上的王报答你的殷勤好客!

我在这里已美美地度过一周。

要不是明天得上路,这你清楚,

我真想在此做你的臣属。

不知你是否真的愿意为我找个向导,

把我带到绿色教堂,让我在新年这天

一任上帝的旨意接受命运的裁决。"

"我真心诚意! "主人说,"请你相信,

凡是我答应过的一切,我坚决履行。"

他即刻为他派定一位仆从,

责成他为高文在山上带路,

Faring through forest and thicket by the most straightforward route

    They might.

    With every honour due

    Gawain then thanked the knight,

    And having bid him adieu,

    Took leave of the ladies bright.

79

SO he spoke to them sadly, sorrowing as he kissed,

And urged on them heartily his endless thanks,

And they gave to Sir Gawain words of grace in return,

Commending him to Christ with cries of chill sadness.

Then from the whole household he honourably took his leave,

Making all the men that he met amends

For their several services and solicitous care,

For they had been busily attendant, bustling about him;

And every soul was as sad to say farewell

As if they had always had the hero in their house.

Then the lords led him with lights to his chamber,

And blithely brought him to bed to rest.

If he slept—I dare not assert it—less soundly than usual,

There was much on his mind for the morrow, if he meant to give

尽可能从最近便的路径穿过

森林和山谷。

高文爵士恭恭敬敬，

衷心感谢城堡骑士，

他向他说了声再见，

同时辞别了众女士。

79

他向她们吻别，心里好不悲伤，

口中不断地道谢，诚意一目了然。

他们以优雅的言辞回答高文，

怀着淡淡的忧虑为他向主颂扬。

然后他又向全城堡的人热情话别，

向所有他遇见的人亲切道谢，

因为他们曾给过他周到的服务，

为照料他忙得不亦乐乎。

每个人跟他告别时都很伤心，

好像英雄本来就是自家人。

然后他们提着灯把他引进卧房，

高高兴兴带他上床休息。

如果他睡着了——我不敢肯定—定睡不香，

但明天的事一旦考虑，免不了千头万绪

It thought.

Let him lie there still,

He almost has what he sought;

So tarry a while until

The process I report.

涌上心头。
就让他休息一会吧，
要找的几乎已找到；
让我就此把笔搁下，
以后的事再做报道。

FIT IV

80

NOW the New Year neared, the night passed,

Daylight fought darkness as the Deity ordained.

But wild was the weather the world awoke to;

Bitterly the clouds cast down cold on the earth,

Inflicting on the flesh flails from the north.

Bleakly the snow blustered, and beasts were frozen;

The whistling wind wailed from the heights,

Driving great drifts deep in the dales.

Keenly the lord listened as he lay in his bed;

Though his lids were closed, he was sleeping little.

Every cock that crew recalled to him his tryst.

Before the day had dawned, he had dressed himself,

For the light from a lamp illuminated his chamber.

He summoned his servant, who swiftly answered,

Commanded that his mail-coat and mount's saddle he brought.

The man fared forth and fetched him his armour,

第四章

80

新年即将来临,前夜已经过去,
白昼秉承神意战胜了黑暗。
恶劣的天气即将把大地唤醒;
寒冷的乌云覆盖苍穹,
北方来风鞭笞人间生灵。
大雪纷纷而下,动物都已冻僵;
呼啸的风在山顶上悲鸣,
卷起峡谷中厚厚的积叶。
骑士躺在床上聆听这一切,
虽然合着双眼,但难以入眠。
每一声公鸡的啼叫都提醒他这次约会。
天未破晓,他已穿衣起床,
因为有灯的光芒把卧室照亮。
他呼唤仆人,仆人立刻回应,
他吩咐他拿来盔甲和马鞍。
仆人遵命行事,递过他的战甲,

And set Sir Gawain's array in splendid style.

First he clad him in his clothes to counter the cold,

Then in his other armour which had been well kept;

His breast- and belly-armour had been burnished bright,

And the rusty rings of his rich mail-coat rolled clean,

And all being as fresh as at first, he was fain to give thanks

    Indeed.

    Each wiped and polished piece

    He donned with due heed.

    The gayest from here to Greece,

    The strong man sent for his steed.

81

WHILE he was putting on apparel of the most princely kind—

His surcoat, with its symbol of spotless deeds

Environed on velvet with virtuous gems,

Was embellished and bound with embroidered seams,

And finely fur-lined with the fairest skins—

He did not leave the lace belt, they lady's gift:

For his own good, Gawain did not forget that!

When he had strapped the sword on his swelling hips,

The knight lapped his loins with his love-token twice,

Quickly wrapped it with relish round his waist.

帮助他穿戴得整整齐齐。
只见他内穿御寒的冬衣,
外面披挂一套预先备下的盔甲,
胸甲和护腰闪闪发光,
上面的铁环被磨得锃亮。
这一切都崭新如故,高文为此
            十分感激。
        他把那副锃亮的盔甲,
        一件件认真地穿起,
        快活的勇士满面春风,
        让仆人牵过他的坐骑。

当他穿上那套华丽的服装——
披上那件象征纯洁的外衣,
天鹅绒上缀满贵重的宝石,
那饰边全都是刺绣的活计,
沿着边缝露出珍贵的毛皮——
他没有留下那根腰带——夫人的礼物:
为了他自己,他不能把它忘记!
当骑士在胯下系上宝剑,
随即兴致勃勃地把爱情信物
绑上腰间,而且一连扎了两圈。

The green silken girdle suited the gallant well,

Backed by the royal red cloth that richly showed.

But Gawain wore the girdle not for its great value,

Nor through pride in the pendants, in spite of their polish,

Nor for the gleaming gold which glinted on the ends,

But to save himself when of necessity he must

Stand an evil stroke, not resisting it with knife

     Or sword.

    When ready and robed aright,

    Out came the comely lord;

    To the men of name and might

    His thanks in plenty poured.

82

Then was Gringolet got ready, that great huge horse.

Having been assiduously stabled in seemly quarters,

The fiery steed was fit and fretting for a gallop.

Sir Gawain stepped to him and, inspecting his coat,

Said earnestly to himself, asserting with truth,

'Here in this castle is a company whose conduct is honourable.

The man who maintains them, may he have joy!

The delightful lady, love befall her while she lives!

Thus for charity they cherish a chance guest

鲜艳的红布衬托出绿色的丝带，
这副打扮与爵士相得益彰。
高文系上这腰带并非因为珍贵，
并非得意于那华美的流苏，
更不是为了炫耀两端闪亮的金子，
他系上它完全为了保护自己，
因为他不得用刀剑，不做抵抗，承受
　　　可怕的一斧。
　　当他把自己穿戴整齐，
　　英俊的骑士走出卧房；
　　滔滔不绝的感激之辞，
　　送给杰出勇敢的一班。

82

高大的名驹格林哥莱也已安好鞍鞯，
这神骏在马厩受到细心照料，
此刻正急切想驰骋疆场。
高文走到它跟前，检查马鞍，
然后用明确的口吻对自己说：
"这座城堡的居民行为可敬，
但愿管辖他们的人幸福无边。
只要活着，快活的夫人将永远享受爱情!
他们对陌生的客人如此好客，

Honourably and open-handedly; may He on high,

The King of Heaven, requite you and your company too!

And if I could live any longer in lands on earth,

Some rich recompense, if I could, I should readily give you."

Then he stepped into the stirrup and swung aloft.

His man showed him his shield; on his shoulder he put it,

And gave the spur to Gringolet with his gold-spiked heels.

The horse sprang forward from the paving, pausing no more

     To prance.

   His man was mounted and fit,

   Laden with spear and lance.

   "This castle to Christ I commit:

   May He its fortune enhance!"

83

THE drawbridge was let down and the broad double gates

Were unbarred and borne open on both sides.

Passing over the planks, the prince blessed himself

And praised the kneeling porter, who proffered him "Good day",

Praying God to grant that Gawain would be saved.

And Gawain went on his way with the one man

To put him on the right path for that perilous place

Where the sad assault must be received by him.

但愿高高在上的主，天上的王，

以同样的方式给他们慷慨的报答！

只要我活在世上，只要可能，

我一定心甘情愿以厚礼偿还！"

说完他跨上马镫，走了一圈，

仆人[22]递过圆盾；他把它挂上肩，

然后就用镶金的踢马刺踢坐骑。

骏马从大道上一跃而起，不停地

　　　向前奔驰。

　　仆人也上了马背，

　　手中提着他的长矛。

　　"我要向基督祈祷，

　　愿主保佑这座城堡。"

83

哨兵为他们放下吊桥，

高大的城门被拔去插销，两边洞开。

过了吊桥，爵士在胸前画了十字，

称赞向他恭敬问候的哨兵，

他祈求上帝保佑自己性命无虞。

然后骑士与他的向导拍马上路，

那向导负责把他带往险地，

在那里接受不幸的一击。

By bluffs where boughs were bare they passed,

Climbed by cliffs where the cold clung:

Under the high clouds, ugly mists

Merged damply with the moors and melted on the mountains;

Each hill had a hat, a huge mantle of mist.

Brooks burst forth above them, boiling over their banks

And showering down sharply in shimmering cascades.

Wonderfully wild was their way through the woods;

Till soon the sun in the sway of that season

     Brought day.

    They were on a lofty hill

    Where snow beside them lay,

    When the servant stopped still

    And told his master to stay.

84

"FOR I have guided you to this ground, Sir Gawain, at this time,

And now you are not far from the noted place

Which you have searched for and sought with such special zeal.

But I must say to you, forsooth, since I know you,

And you are a lord whom I love with no little regard:

Take my governance as guide, and it shall go better for you,

For the place is perilous that you are pressing towards.

沿途悬崖上树木光秃萧疏，
严寒在峭壁上久久留驻：
广阔的云天下，邪恶的湿雾
弥漫在沼泽地，消散在山冈，
每座小山都披上了浓雾的外氅。
溪水在雾气中奔流，溢出堤岸，
白茫茫的瀑布直泻而下。
林间的道路极其荒凉，
太阳在季节的更替中

    捎上天光。

   他们登上一个山巅，

   脚下堆着厚厚积雪，

   仆人勒马不再前进，

   告诉主人停下脚步。

84

"高文爵士，我已把你带到此地，
你那么热心寻找的地方
已离这里不远。我必须对你说，
真的，自从我认识你，
我一直把你当作我最敬重的人。
请你听我的话，这对你有好处，
你急切寻找的地方充满凶险。

In that wilderness dwells the worst man in the world,

For he is valiant and fierce and fond of fighting,

And mightier than any man that may be on earth,

And his body is bigger than the best four

In Arthur's house, or Hector, or any other.

At the Green Chapel he gains his great adventures.

No man passes that place, however proud in arms,

Without being dealt a death-blow by his dreadful hand.

For he is an immoderate man, to mercy a stranger;

For whether churl or chaplain by the chapel rides,

Monk or mass-priest or man of other kind,

He thinks it as convenient to kill him as keep alive himself.

Therefore I say, as certainly as you sit in your saddle,

If you come there you'll be killed, I caution you, knight,

Take my troth for it, though you had twenty lives

       And more.

    He has lived here since long ago

    And filled the field with gore.

    You cannot counter his blow,

    It strikes so sudden and sore."

85

'THERERORE, good Sir Gawain, leave the grim man alone!

世上最邪恶的人居住在那片荒野。

他好勇斗狠,热衷于战争,

人世间没有人比他更强悍,

他的身躯比亚瑟宫廷四杰还高大

甚至超过赫克托,或其他任何人。

他在绿色教堂过着冒险生活。

任何人经过那里,不管如何善战,

都逃脱不了他致命的一击。

他是个狂徒,对陌生人从不讲怜悯。

谁要是骑马而过,不管是农夫还是牧师,

传教士还是弥撒主持,或者别的什么人,

他都会轻而易举把他杀死。

因此我要给你说句大实话,

如果你去那里,骑士,你必然被杀,

我提醒你,相信我的话吧,因为你

   年纪尚轻。

  他居住那里已经很久,

  这一带遍地血腥,

  你无法抵抗他的斧头,

  它来势凶猛,既快又狠。"

85

"因此,高文爵士,别理会这个凶人!

Ride by another route, to some region remote!

Go in the name of God, and Christ grace your fortune!

And I shall go home again and undertake

To swear solemnly by God and his saints as well

(By my halidom, so help me God, and every other oath)

Stoutly to keep your secret, not saying to a soul

That ever you tried to turn tail from any man I knew."

"Great thanks," replied Gawain, somewhat galled, and said,

"It is worthy of you to wish for my well-being, man,

And I believe you would loyally lock it in your heart.

But however quiet you kept it, if I quit this place,

Fled from the fellow in the fashion you propose,

I should become a cowardly knight with no excuse whatever,

For I will go to the Green Chapel, to get what Fate sends,

And have whatever words I wish with that worthy,

Whether weal or woe is what Fate

      Demands.

   Fierce though that fellow be,

   Clutching his club where he stands,

   Our Lord can certainly see

   That his own are in safe hands."

走另外一条路,看在上帝的分上,
远远地避开他! 基督保佑你平安无事!
我这就骑马回家,凭着上帝和圣徒
我庄严地发誓(上帝为我做证,
我决不会违背自己的诺言):
我要严守秘密,决不会跟任何人说起
你曾经临阵脱逃,不敢去会什么人。"
"谢谢你,"有些恼怒的高文回答,
"难为你为我着想,伙计,
我相信你会为我严守秘密。
然而,如果我离开这里,按照你的建议
避开那位骑士,不管你如何保持沉默,
我都将成为毋庸争辩的懦夫。
我现在一定要去一趟绿色教堂,
让命运之神做出安排,不管是祸是福,
都要去听听那位大名鼎鼎的人物
　　　　　说话的声音。
　　　尽管那家伙凶狠无比,
　　　手提着棍棒虎视眈眈,
　　　我们的主一定会庇护,
　　　让他的子民安然无恙。"

86

"BY Mary!" said the other man, "If you mean what you say,
You are determined to take all your trouble on yourself.
If you wish to lose your life, I'll no longer hinder you.
Here's your lance for your hand, your helmet for your head.
Ride down this rough track round younder cliff
Till you arrive in a rugged ravine at the bottom,
Then look about on the flat, on your left hand,
And you will view there in the vale that very chapel,
And the grim gallant who guards it always.
Now, noble Gawain, good-bye in God's name.
For all the gold on God's earth I would not go with you,
Nor foot it an inch further through this forest as your fellow."
Whereupon he wrenched at his reins, that rider in the woods,
Hit the horse with his heels as hard as he could,
Sent him leaping along, and left the knight there
      Alone.
    "By God!" said Gawain, "I swear
    I will not weep or groan:
    Being given to God's good care,
    My trust in Him shall be shown."

86

"天哪！"向导说，"如果你一意孤行，
那你无疑是在找自己的麻烦。
如果你一心求死，我也不必再劝你。
请接住这把长矛，戴上这顶头盔。
沿着这条崎岖的小道绕过那边悬崖，
直到进入下面树木茂密的深谷，
然后在一方平地上向左边张望，
你就能看见深谷中那座教堂，
凶恶的骑士一直在那里站岗。
高贵的高文，让我们就此分手吧，
哪怕世上的黄金全归我，我也不想与你同行，
不想作为你的伙伴再迈进森林一步。"
说完，这骑手在林间猛一转身，
用马刺使劲踢了踢坐骑，
让它奋蹄而去，将高文一人
          抛在背后。
      "上帝做证，"高文说，
      "我决不哭泣哀叹，
      我受主悉心照拂，
      我对他信任昭然。"

209

87

THEN he gave the spur to Gringolet and galloped down the path,

Thrust through a thicket there by a bank,

And rode down the rough slope right into the ravine.

Then he searched about, but it seemed savage and wild,

And no sign did he see of any sort of building;

But on both sides banks, beetling and steep,

And great crooked crags, cruelly jagged;

The bristling barbs of rock seemed to brush the sky.

Then he held in his horse, halted there,

Scanned on every side in search of the chapel.

He saw no such thing anywhere, which seemed remarkable,

Save, hard by in the open, a hillock of sorts,

A smooth-surfaced barrow on slope beside a stream

Which flowed forth fast there in its course,

Foaming and frothing as if feverishly boiling.

The knight, urging his horse, pressed onwards to the mound,

Dismounted manfully and made fast to a lime-tree

The reins, hooking them round a rough branch;

Then he went to the barrow, which he walked round, inspecting,

Wondering what in the world it might be.

It had a hole in each end and on either side,

87

然后他一踢格林哥莱冲下山道，
跨过堤岸边一丛茂密的灌木，
沿着山坡而下，一直进入峡谷。
他环顾四周，只见那里一片荒芜，
并没有任何建筑的迹象。
峡谷两侧地势险峻，起伏不平。
巨大的峭壁似乎在擦刷天际。
他勒住骏马，在那里停下，
审视四周以寻找绿色教堂。
他没有发现类似教堂的任何房屋，
除了附近开阔处有一座小山，
斜坡上有座表面平整的墓冢，
旁边一条小溪急急奔流向前，
泡沫飞溅，好像溪水正在沸腾。
骑士催马来到墓冢边，
利索地下了马，把马拴在菩提树下，
马缰绳绕住弯曲的树枝。
然后他走近墓冢，围着它观察，
好奇那里面会有什么怪物。
墓冢前后左右都有一个洞，
周围长满大片茂密的野草。

And was overgrown with grass in great patches.

All hollow it was within, only an old cavern

Or the crevice of an ancient crag: he could not explain it

      Aright.

    "O God, is the Chapel Green

    This mound?" said the noble knight.

    "At such might Satan be seen

    Saying matins at midnight."

88

"NOW certainly the place is deserted," said Gawain,

"It is a hideous oratory, all overgrown,

And well graced for the gallant garbed in green

To deal out his devotions in the Devil's fashion.

Now I feel in my five wits, it is the Fiend himself

That has tricked me into this tryst, to destroy me here.

This is a chapel of mischance—checkmate to it!

It is the most evil holy place I ever entered."

With his high helmet on his head, and holding his lance,

He roamed up to the roof of that rough dwelling.

Then from that height he heard, from a hard rock

On the bank beyond the brook, a barbarous noise.

What! It clattered amid the cliffs fit to cleave them apart,

洞里空空荡荡,墓冢像一个古穴,
或者峭壁中一个裂口:高文难以
　　　　将其解释。
　　"天哪,"高尚的骑士自问,
　　"难道墓冢就是教堂?
　　如果是,那我可以看见
　　撒旦在午夜做晨祷了。"

88

"这座墓冢显然已荒废,"高文说,
"它野草丛生,是一座丑陋的教堂,
那穿绿衣的骑士真够幸运,
竟然以魔鬼的面目在此安身。
我凭五智感到,是撒旦自己
骗我来此约会,企图把我毁灭。
这是一所不祥的教堂——实在该死!
我走进了最邪恶的圣地。"
骑士头戴头盔,手握长矛
在荒草丛生的墓冢上踱步。
这时,突然听见一个粗野的声音
来自头顶,来自小溪对面的岩石。
哇! 那声音足以使山崖为之开裂,

As if a great scythe were being ground on a grindstone there.

What! It whirred and it whetted like water in a mill.

What! It made a rushing, ringing din, rueful to hear.

"By God!" then said Gawain, "that is going on,

I suppose, as a salute to myself, to greet me

  Hard by.

  God's will be warranted:

  'Alas!' is a craven cry.

  No din shall make me dread

  Although today I die."

89

THEN the courteous knight called out clamorously,

"Who holds sway here and has an assignation with me?

For the good knight Gawain is on the ground here.

If anyone there wants anything, wend your way hither fast,

And further your needs either now, or not at all."

"Bide there!" said one on the bank above his head,

"And you shall swiftly receive what I once swore to give you."

Yet for a time he continued his tumult of scraping,

Turning away as he whetted, before he would descend.

Then he thrust himself round a thick crag through a hole,

Whirling round a wedge of rock with a frightful weapon,

如同大镰刀在磨刀石上磨砺，
如同磨坊里的水在回旋撞击，
它构成一阵轰鸣，使人毛骨悚然。
"我的天！"高文说，"刚才的声音，
我猜想，是向我表示敬意，对我表示
　　　隆重欢迎。
　　上帝可以为我担保：
　　只有懦夫才会慌神。
　　任何声音吓我不倒，
　　即使我丧命在今朝。"

89

彬彬有礼的骑士于是大声发问：
"谁在这里？谁跟我相约？
骑士高文现在就站在这里，
如果你有什么要求，请赶快过来，
要么现在就提，要么永远闭嘴！"
"你等着！"来自头顶的声音说，
"你马上能得到我曾经答应过的一切。"
对方仍未露面，在他下山以前，
继续弄出一阵喧嚣的声响。
最后他才从一个岩洞里钻出，
手提一柄锋利的丹麦斧子，

A Danish axe duly honed for dealing the blow,

With a broad biting edge, bow-bent along the handle,

Ground on a grindstone, a great four-foot blade—

No less, by that love-lace gleaming so brightly!

And the gallant in green was garbed as at first,

His looks and limbs the same, his locks and beard;

Save that steadily on his feet he strode on the ground,

setting the handle to the stony earth and stalking beside it.

He would not wade through the water when he came to it,

But vaulted over on his axe, then with huge strides

Advanced violently and fiercely along the field's width

On the snow.

Sir Gawain went to greet

The knight, not bowing low.

The man said, "Sir so sweet,

You honour the trysts you owe."

90

"GAWAIN," said the green knight, "may God guard you!

You are welcome to my dwelling, I warrant you,

And you have timed your travel here as a true man ought.

You know plainly the pact we pledged between us:

This time a twelvemonth ago you took your portion,

旋风般绕过一根石柱。

锋利的斧刃,边长足有四英尺,

其长度不亚于那根象征爱情的腰带,

它明晃晃的像一张大弓安在斧柄上。

绿衣骑士的穿着一如当初,

那神态、头发和胡须也是先前模样。

只是这一次他昂首阔步走在地上,

手中的斧柄碰击着多石地面。

过小溪时他没有蹚水,

而是撑住斧柄一跃而过。

他来势汹汹,大踏步穿过雪地,来到
　　　　高文跟前。

　　　高文没有被他吓住,

　　　他过去迎接这绿衣人。

　　　对方说:"可爱的爵士,

　　　你如期赴约为人真诚。"

90

"高文,"绿衣骑士说,"愿上帝保佑你!

欢迎你来到我的居住地,我向你保证,

你如期赴约,是个真正的男子汉。

我们之间立下的誓约你很清楚:

一年前这个时候你行使了你的权利,

And now at his New Year I should nimbly requite you.

And we are on our own here in this valley

With no seconds to sunder us, spar as we will.

Take your helmet off your head, and have your payment here.

And offer no more argument or action than I did

When you whipped off my head with one stroke."

"No," said Gawain, "by God who gave me a soul,

The grievous gash to come I grudge you not at all;

Strike but the one stroke and I shall stand still

And offer you no hindrance; you may act freely,

     I swear."

   Head bent, Sir Gawain bowed,

   And showed the bright flesh bare.

   He behaved as if uncowed,

   Being loth to display his care.

91

THEN the gallant in green quickly got ready,

Heaved his horrid weapon on high to hit Gawain,

With all the brute force in his body bearing it aloft,

Swinging savagely enough to strike him dead.

Had it driven down as direly as he aimed,

The daring dauntless man would have died from the blow.

218

今年元旦我将以同样的方式回报你。

没有助手把我们分开，或代替我们比赛。

把头盔摘下吧，我这就还你一斧。

用不着多说，用不着再等，

就像当初你一斧砍下我的头颅。"

"好吧，"高文说，"凭赋予我灵魂的上帝做证，

我毫不妒忌这一斧轮到了你砍。

砍吧，但只能一斧，我将站着不动，

不做任何抵抗，我保证你

　　　　行动自由。"

　　高文于是把头低垂，

　　让雪白的皮肉裸露，

　　看样子他视死如归，

　　不肯流露半点怯懦。

91

绿衣骑士很快做好准备，

对准高文把可怕的斧子高高举起，

全身的气力全使到了斧子上，

只等猛力一挥，置人死地。

如果他这一斧砍准了，

无所畏惧的人必死无疑。

But Gawain glanced up at the grim axe beside him

As it came shooting through the shivering air to shatter him,

And his shoulders shrank slightly from the sharp edge.

The other suddenly stayed the descending axe,

And then reproved the prince with many proud words:

"You are not Gawain," said the gallant, "whose greatness is such

That by hill or hollow no army ever frightened him;

For now you flinch for fear before you feel harm.

I never did know that knight to be a coward.

I neither flinched nor fled when you let fly your blow,

Nor offered any quibble in the house of King Arthur.

My head flew to my feet, but flee I did not.

Yet you quail cravenly though unscathed so far.

So I am bound to be called the better man

      Therefore."

    Said Gawain, "Not again

    Shall I flinch as I did before;

    But if my head pitch to the plain,

    It's off for evermore."

92

"BUT be brisk, man, by your faith, and bring me to the point;

Deal me my destiny and do it out of hand,

但当斧子从颤抖的空气中落下，
高文抬头看了一眼可怕的凶器，
他的肩膀缩了缩，正好躲过斧刃。
绿衣骑士即刻收住斧子，
以傲慢的语言责备他。
"你不是那个伟大的高文，"他说，
"高文冲锋陷阵，战场上不怕任何人，
没想到此人竟是个胆小鬼。
在亚瑟的宫廷，当你的斧子砍下来，
我既没退缩、躲避，也没争辩。
当我的头落地，我仍不逃走。
而你却不待斧子砍下就胆怯地退缩。
比较我们两人，显然还是我
　　　　更加勇敢。"
　　"请你放心，"高文回答，
　　"我绝对不会再躲避；
　　但我的头一旦落下，
　　将永远与躯体分离。"

92

　　"爽快点，伙计，一定要砍准，
　　我的命运掌握在你手里，请马上动手，

For I shall stand your stroke, not starting at all

Till your axe has hit me. Here is my oath on it."

"Have at you then!" said the other, heaving up his axe,

Behaving as angrily as if he were mad.

He menaced him mightily, but made no contact,

Smartly withholding his hand without hurting him.

Gawain waited unswerving, with not a wavering limb,

But stood still as a a stone or the stump of a tree

Gripping the rocky ground with a hundred grappling roots.

Then again the green knight began to gird:

"So now you have a whole heart I must hit you.

May the high knighthood which Arthur conferred

Preserve you and save your neck, if so it avail you!"

Then said Gawain, storming with sudden rage,

"Thrash on, you thrustful fellow, you threaten too much.

It seems your spirit is struck with self-dread."

"Forsooth," the other said, "You speak so fiercely

I will no longer lengthen matters by delaying your business,

  I vow."

 He stood astride to smite,

 Lip pouting, puckered brow.

 No wonder he lacked delight

 Who expected no help now.

我站着等你,决不挪动一步,
直到斧子砍中我。这是我的誓言。”
“那就砍吧!”骑士说完举起斧子,
气势汹汹的样子好像气得发了狂。
他极力恐吓他,但斧子没碰着,
他敏捷地缩回手,没把高文伤害。
高文等待着,身子一动不动,
就好像他是一块磐石,或一棵树,
千百条根须把多石地面紧紧扎住。
绿衣骑士再次挖苦他:
“即使你有十足的勇气,我也要砍你,
但愿亚瑟王授予你的骑士称号
能保住你的脖子,如果它真有妙用!”
高文听后勃然大怒,他说:
“快砍吧,你这狂徒,你恐吓够了!
看样子是你自己心里发虚。”
“你说话真的太不客气了,”另一个回答,
“我发誓,这回我不再拖延,马上跟你
　　把账清算。”
　他叉开两腿站着,
　噘起嘴,皱紧眉头。
　难怪高文不快活,
　此刻他无人能救。

93

UP went the axe at once and hurtled down straight

At the naked neck with its knife-like edge.

Though it swung down savagely, slight was the wound,

A mere snick on the side, so that the skin was broken.

Through the fair fat to the flesh fell the blade,

And over his shoulders the shimmering blood shot to the ground.

When Sir Gawain saw his gore glinting on the snow,

He leapt feet close together a spear's length away,

Hurriedly heaved his helmet on to his head,

And shrugging his shoulders, shot his shield to the front,

Swung out his bright sword and said fiercely,

(For never had the knight since being nursed by his mother

Been so buoyantly happy, so blithe in this world)

"Cease your blows, sir, strike me no more.

I have sustained a stroke here unresistingly,

And if you offer any more I shall earnestly reply.

Resisting, rest assured, with the most rancorous

      Despite.

    The single stroke is wrought

    To which we pledged our plight

    In high King Arthur's court:

93

骑士突然举起斧子,锋利的斧刃
对准裸露的脖子直砍而下。
然而,来势虽猛,伤势却轻,
只是脖子一侧被划破了一点皮。
斧子没有砍进脂肪和肌肉,
但殷红的血已从肩膀流到地上。
高文看见自己的血滴落雪地,
即刻一跃而起,跳出一枪杆远,
急急忙忙把头盔戴上,
耸耸肩膀,将盾挡在胸前,
抽出闪亮的宝剑厉声说
(凡世上母亲养大的骑士
没有一个能比他更快活、更兴奋):
"停下,骑士,你不能再砍了。
我不做抵抗承受了你一斧,
如果你再砍,我将认真还手。
你可以相信,那时我的反抗将
　　　　不讲情面。
　　去年在亚瑟的宫廷,
　　我们彼此立下誓约,
　　如今这一斧已兑现,

Enough now, therefore, knight!"

94

THE bold man stood back and bent over his axe,

Putting the haft to earth, and leaning on the head.

He gazed at Sir Gawain on the ground before him,

Considering the spirited and stout way he stood,

Audacious in arms; his heart warmed to him.

Then he gave utterance gladly in his great voice,

With resounding speech saying to the knight,

"Bold man, do not be so bloodily resolute.

No one here has offered you evil discourteously,

Contrary to the covenant made at the King's court.

I promised a stroke, which you received: consider yourself paid.

I cancel all other obligations of whatever kind.

If I had been more active, perhaps I could

Have made you suffer by striking a savager stroke.

First in foolery I made a feint at srtiking,

Not rending you with a riving cut—and right I was,

On a account of the first night's covenant we accorded;

For you truthfully kept your trust in troth with me,

Giving me your gains, as a good man should.

The further feinted blow was for the following day,

骑士,你所得已够多。"

94

勇敢的骑士退后一步,放下斧子,
斧柄插在地上,身子斜靠一旁,
他凝视着站在面前的高文,
心里想着他的坚强与勇敢,
不知不觉对他产生了好感。
他显得高兴,用洪亮的声音
对高文爵士说了以下一番话:
"勇士,用不着如此气势汹汹,
与在亚瑟宫廷的情景相反,
这里不再有人向你表示恶意。
我答应还你一斧,你已经得到:
事情已经了结,我不再有其他要求。
如果我存心害你,也许我能够
让你蒙受更惨重的打击。
第一斧我只是佯装攻击,
没有砍下你的头——这我有自己的理由,
因为头天晚上的契约你已遵守。
你说话算数,对我讲究信用,
像一个真正的男子汉将所获交出。
第二次佯攻则针对第二天的事,

When you kissed my comely wife, and the kisses came to me:

For those two things, harmlessly I thrust twice at you

       Feinted blows.

    Truth for truth's the word;

    No need for dread, God knows.

    From your failure at the third

    The tap you took arose.

95

"FOR that braided belt you wear belongs to me.

I am well aware that my own wife gave it you.

Your conduct and your kissings are completely known to me,

And the wooing by my wife—my work set it on.

I instructed her to try you, and you truly seem

To be the most perfect paladin ever to pace the earth.

As the pearl to the white pea in precious worth,

So in good faith is Gawain to other gay knights.

But here your faith failed you, you flagged somewhat, sir,

Yet it was not for a well-wrought thing, nor for wooing either,

But for love of your life, which is less blameworthy."

The other strong man stood considering this a while,

So filled with fury that his flesh trembled,

And the blood from his breast burst forth in his face

我美丽的妻子吻了你，你则把吻送还我：

为这两回，我佯攻了你两次，每次都

不伤着你。

这叫作以真诚换真诚，

上帝确保你无忧无患；

但因你第三次失了信，

导致这会儿蒙受轻伤。

95

"你身上系的腰带是我的物品。

我知道是我妻子把它赠送给你。

你们亲吻的事我全都清楚，

还有我妻的求爱——全出于我的安排。

我让她试探你，但你证明自己

是普天之下最完美的骑士。

你与其他快活的骑士相比，

那价值就如珍珠之于豌豆。

但这次你失了信，完美由此打了折扣。

不过，你不是出于激情或求爱，

而是因为热爱生命，这也就情有可原。"

另一位勇士站着认真思索，

禁不住浑身颤抖，又恼又恨，

热血在周身沸腾，白脸变成了红脸，

229

As he shrank for shame at what the chevalier spoke of.

The first words the fair knight could frame were:

"Curses on both cowardice and covetousness!

Their vice and villainy are virtue's undoing."

Then he took the knot, with a twist twitched it loose,

And fiercely flung the fair girdle to the knight.

"Lo! There is the false thing, foul fortune befall it!

I was craven about our encounter, and cowardice taught me

To accord with covetousness and corrupt my nature

And the liberality and loyalty belonging to chivalry.

Now I am faulty and false and found fearful always.

In the train of treachery and untruth go woe

      And shame.

    I acknowledge, knight, how ill

    I behaved, and take the blame.

    Award what penance you will:

    Henceforth I'll shun ill-fame."

96

THEN the other lord laughed and politely said,

"In my view you have made amends for your misdemeanour;

You have confessed your faults fully with fair acknowledgement,

And plainly done penance at the point of my axe.

因为他对骑士所言深感羞愧。
高文能说出的第一句话是：
"怯懦和贪婪都应受到诅咒，
两者的罪过都是美德的对头。"
然后他一挥手解下身上的腰带，
狠狠地把它丢还给绿衣骑士：
"接住！这不吉的东西，愿厄运降临它！
我渴求这次会面，但怯懦教唆我
与贪婪结盟，玷污了我的品德，
败坏了骑士的慷慨与忠诚。
如今我品德受损，成了一介懦夫。
背信弃义造成的恶果必将是
　　　　　悲伤与羞辱。
　　我承认自己罪孽深重，
　　骑士，你就谴责我吧。
　　任凭你判我如何赎罪，
　　从今后我将避开恶名。"

96

另一位骑士哈哈大笑，他礼貌地说：
"在我看来你已弥补了自己的过失，
你已坦诚地供认了自己的罪过，
我的斧子也履行了惩戒的职责，

You are absolved of your sin and as stainless now

As if you had never fallen in fault since first you were born.

As for the gold-hemmed girdle, I give it you, sir,

Seeing it is as green as my gown. Sir Gawain, you may

Think about this trial when you throng in company

With paragons of princes, for it is a perfect token,

At knightly gatherings, of the great adventrue at the Green
   Chapel.

You shall come back to my castle this cold New Year,

And we shall revel away the rest of this rich feast;

> Let us go."

> Thus urging him, the lord

> Said, "You and my wife, I know

> We shall bring to clear accord,

> Though she was your fierce foe."

97

"NO, forsooth," said the knight, seizing his helmet,

And doffing it with dignity as he delivered this thanks,

"My stay has sufficed me. Still, luck go with you!

May He who bestows all good, honour you with it!

And commend me to the courteous lady, your comely wife;

Indeed, my due regards to both dear ladies,

你如今已获赦免,清白如故,
就好像生下后从未犯过错误。
至于这条金丝腰带,我把它送给你,
由于它与我的服饰同色。高文爵士,
当你与一班王公贵族待在一起,
它能使你想起这次试探,作为完美的见证,
说明你在绿色教堂有过冒险历程。
现在请你返回我的城堡,
一起欢度这寒冷的元旦节。

　　　　　我们上路吧。"

　　城堡主这样催促他,

　　　"我知道,我们还得费神

　　　让你和我的妻子和解,

　　　虽然她是你的仇人。"

97

"我不去了,"骑士说,一边脱下头盔,
恭恭敬敬地向城堡主表示感谢。
"我已住得很满意。愿你好运!
愿赋予一切的主给你带来荣耀!
请代我向你好客的夫人致意,
噢,我的问候应给予两位夫人,

Who with their wanton wiles have thus waylaid their knight.

But it is no marvel for a foolish man to be maddened thus

And saddled with sorrow by the sleights of women.

For here on earth was Adam taken in by one,

And Solomon by many such, and Samson likewise;

Delilah dealt him his doom; and David, later still,

Was blinded by Bathsheba, and badly suffered for it.

Since these were troubled by their tricks, it would be true joy

To love them but not believe them, if a lord could,

For these were the finest of former times, most favoured by fortune

Of all under the heavenly kingdom whose hearts were

     Abused;

    These four all fell to schemes

    Of women whom they used.

    If I am snared, it seems

    I ought to be excused.

98

"BUT your girdle," said Gawain, "God requite you for it!

Not for the glorious gold shall I gladly wear it,

Nor for the stuff nor the silk nor the swaying pendants,

Nor for its worth, fine workmanship or wonderful honour;

But as a sign of my sin I shall see it often,

是她俩设计捉弄我这位骑士。
愚蠢的男人被女人的诡计折腾得发狂，
陷入无穷的悲伤，那也不是什么怪事。
亚当就曾经上过一个女人的当，
所罗门则多次受骗，参孙也一样，
大利拉要了他的命。后来还有大卫，
他被拔示巴所迷，结果吃足了苦头。
既然他们都难免上当，对于男人来说，
爱她们就是幸福，但不可给予信任，
这些滥用感情的人都是古代英豪，
他们在天地间曾受到命运之神
　　　　　特别宠信。
　　这四位伟人无一例外，
　　都上过所爱女人的当；
　　假如我真的上了圈套，
　　似乎也应该得到原谅。"

98

"至于那根腰带，"高文说，"主报答你的好意!
我乐意系上它不是为贪图上面的黄金，
不是为那丝绸料子或飘动的流苏，
不是为它的价值，做工或什么荣耀，
而是作为罪孽的象征以便我经常看见。

Remembering with remorse, when I am mounted in glory,

The fault and faintheartedness of the perverse flesh,

How it tends to attract tarnishing sin.

So when pride shall prick me for my prowess in arms,

One look at this love-lace will make lowly my heart.

But one demand I make of you, may it not incommode you:

Since you are master of the demesne I have remained in a while,

Make known, by your knighthood—and now may He above,

Who sits on high and holds up heaven, requite you!—

How you pronounce your true name; and no more request."

"Truly," the other told him, "I shall tell you my title.

Bertilak of the High Desert I am called here in this land.

Through the might of Morgan the Fay, who remains in my house,

Through the wiles of her witchcraft, a lore well learned—

Many of the magical arts of Merlin she acquired,

For she lavished fervent love long ago

On that susceptible sage: certainly your knights know

      Of their fame.

  So 'Morgan the Goddess'

  She accordingly became;

  The proudest she can oppress

  And to her pupose tame—"

当我光荣地跨上战马，它能使我
怀着悔恨想起肉体的缺陷与弱点，
记住它如何易于招致污秽的罪恶。
这样，每当我扬扬得意于非凡的武功，
看一眼这腰带就能使我变得谦恭。
但我还有一个问题，但愿你能回答，
既然你是这里的主人，我又住了这么久，
请你以骑士的名义——但愿天上的主，
统治天界的万能者报答你——
告诉我你的真名。我只有这个要求。"
骑士说："我确实应该把名号告诉你，
这里的人都叫我'大荒野的贝特拉克'，
我们的城堡由仙女摩根创建——
她本人就在那里面——一切由魔法支配，
谁都知道，摩根从梅林那里学到许多东西，
当年她无比慷慨地将热烈的爱
献给那位多情的圣贤：你们骑士一定听说
　　他们的大名。
　　她掌握着种种魔法，
　　就此变成'摩根仙女'，
　　她有能力主宰天下，
　　任意将高傲者驱使。"

99

"SHE sent me forth in this form to your famous hall
To put to the proof the great pride of the house,
The reputation for high renown of the Round Table;
She bewitched me in this werid way to bewilder your wits,
And to grieve Guinevere and goad her to death
With ghastly fear of that ghost's ghoulish speaking
With his head in his hand before the high table.
That is the aged beldame who is at home:
She is indeed your own aunt, Arthur's half-sister,
Daughter of the Duchess of Tintagel who in due course,
By Uther, was mother of Arthur, who now holds sway.
Therefore I beg you, bold sir, come back to your aunt,
Make merry in my house, for my men love you,
And by my faith, brave sir, I bear you as much good will
As I grant any man under God, for your great honesty."
But Gawain firmly refused with a final negative.
They clasped and kissed, commending each other
To the Prince of Paradise, and parted on the cold ground

> Right there.
>> Gawain on steed serene
>> Spurred to court with courage fair,

99

"她派我以这副模样前往你们的宫廷，
看看你们引以为豪的武功是否属实，
圆桌骑士的荣誉是否经得起考验。
她施展魔力，让我迷惑你们的心智，
以便让奎妮佛伤心，让鬼魂在圆桌前
手执自己的头颅，讲出
令人胆寒的话语，以期把她吓死。
她就是城堡里那位年迈的妇人，
其实她是你的姑妈，亚瑟的异父姐姐，
丁塔吉尔公爵夫人的女儿。
公爵夫人后来嫁给尤塞，成了亚瑟的母亲。
因此请求你，骑士，回去见见你的姑妈，
让城堡充满欢乐，因为我的人都爱你，
我向你担保，由于你一片真诚，
我对你像对待任何人一样，只有善意。"
但高文坚决拒绝骑士的邀请。
他们于是拥抱、亲吻，向天上的王
赞美对方的美德，然后就在冰天雪地里
　　　分手告别。
　　高文稳稳跨上坐骑，
　　雄赳赳返回亚瑟宫廷；

And the gallant garbed in green

To wherever he would elsewhere.

NOW Gawain goes riding on Gringolet

In lonely lands, his life saved by grace.

Often he stayed at a house, and often in the open,

And often overcame hazards in the valleys,

Which at this time I do not intend to tell you about.

The hurt he had had in his neck was healed,

And the glittering girdle that girt him round

Obliquely, like a baldric, was bound by his side

And laced under the left arm with a lasting knot,

In token that he was taken in a tarnishing sin;

And so he came to court, quite unscathed.

When the great became aware of Gawain's arrival

There was general jubilation at the joyful news.

The King kissed the knight, and the Queen likewise,

And so did many a staunch noble who sought to salute him.

They all asked him about his expedition,

And he truthfully told them of his tribulations—

What chanced at the chapel, the good cheer of the knight,

The lady's love-making, and lastly, the girdle.

骑士身披绿色外衣，

回到他原先的栖居地。

100

高文骑着格林哥莱行进在寂静原野上，

他的性命终于安然无恙。

他时而投宿客店，时而歇脚露天，

深山峡谷中克服了种种危险，

这一切在此我不想一一细述。

他脖子上的伤口已经愈合，

那根鲜艳的腰带像胸绶

斜挂在胸前，系在他的身侧，

在左胳膊下打下一个结，它标志

他曾上当受骗，犯下有损名誉的罪行。

如今他终于平安回到宫中。

当亚瑟王得知这个消息，

他欣喜万分，心情十分激动。

国王和王后都吻了这位骑士，

许多王公贵族都前来向高文致意。

他们纷纷询问他的冒险经历。

他则如实叙说路途的艰难，

叙说如何找到绿色教堂，骑士如何欢迎他，

女主人如何求爱，最后还说到那根腰带。

He displayed the scar of the snick on his neck

Where the bold man's blow had hit, his bad faith to

        Proclaim;

    He groaned at his disgrace,

    Unfolding his ill-fame,

    And blood suffused his face

    When he showed his mark of shame.

101

"LOOK, my lord," said Gawain, the lace in his hand.

"This belt confirms the blame I bear on my neck,

My bane and debasement, the burden I bear

For being caught by cowardice and covetousness.

This is the figure of the faithlessness found in me,

Which I must needs wear while I live.

For man can conceal sin but not dissever from it,

So when it is once fixed, it will never be worked loose."

First the King, then all the court, comforted the knight,

And all the lords and ladies belonging to the Table

Laughed at it loudly, and concluded amiably

That each brave man of the brotherhood should bear a baldric,

A band, obliquely about him, of bright green,

Of the same hue as Sir Gawain's and for his sake wear it.

他还给大家看脖子上的伤痕，
那是绿衣骑士的斧子留下的痕迹，见证
　　　　他的违信背约。
　　高文为这次耻辱叹息，
　　因为它败坏他的名声。
　　当他出示耻辱的标志，
　　他自己首先涨红了脸。

101

"陛下，你看，"高文手握腰带说，
"就是这根腰带使我的脖子受伤，
使我走向堕落，名誉受损，
它证明我既怯懦又贪心。
它是自食其言的见证，
我必须系上它，只要我活着。
罪恶只要不被发现，人就会隐瞒它，
罪恶一旦形成，就再也不能消除。"
国王和全宫廷的人都安慰高文，
所有的圆桌骑士和夫人小姐
都哈哈大笑，他们亲切地做出决定：
为了高文，每位圆桌骑士
都必须在胸前斜挂一条绶带，
其颜色与高文的腰带相同。

So it ranked as renown to the Round Table,

And an everlasting honour to him who had it,

As is rendered in Romance's rarest book.

Thus in the days of Arthur this exploit was achieved,

To which the books of Brutus bear witness;

After the bold baron, Brutus, came here,

The siege and the assault being ceased at Troy

> Before.

> Such exploits, I'll be sworn,

> Have happened here of yore.

> Now Christ with his crown of thorn

> Bring us his bliss evermore! AMEN

HONY SOYT QUI MAL PENCE

这样,绶带成了圆桌骑士的荣誉,

成了佩戴者光荣的标记,

最好的罗曼史作品都这样描述。

在亚瑟王时代,这次伟绩就这样完成。

有关布鲁图斯的著作都有记载。

此事发生在布鲁图斯国王以后,

而那场围攻特洛伊的战争早已

　　　　熄灭在先。

　　这样的伟绩,我打赌,

　　古时候确实发生过。

　　如今戴荆棘冠的基督,

　　给我们带来幸福! 阿门。

有邪念之人应感到惭愧。

COMMENTS/注释

[1] 指特洛伊英雄安忒诺耳和埃涅阿斯。据流传于中世纪的一些伪古典文献,他们都犯有叛国罪。

[2] 图斯卡尼,现意大利中部地区。

[3] 伦巴第,现意大利北部地区。

[4] 菲勒克斯·布鲁图斯,传说中不列颠王国的开创者。

[5] 凯姆洛特,虚拟的亚瑟宫廷所在地。

[6] 图卢兹,法国南部一城市;突厥斯坦,现我国新疆、中亚各国及阿富汗一带。

[7] 厄尔,英国古代长度单位,约等于45英寸。

[8] 指仆役。

[9] 根据中世纪民俗,用脚去踢被砍下的巫师的头,是为防止它接回身上。

[10] 仄费洛斯,古希腊神话中的西风神。

[11] 格林哥莱,马名。

[12] 同心结,爱情的象征。

[13] 五智,指人的五种才能:判断、想象、幻想、猜测和记忆。

[14] 五大欢喜,指圣母领报、基督诞生、基督复活、基督升天和圣母升天。

[15] 安格尔西、霍利黑德和威勒尔,均为真实地名,在威尔士西北部。

[16] 圣朱利安,旅行者的保护神。

[17] 中世纪曾有用纸剪成城堡图案用来装点食品的风俗,乔叟(1343—1400)在其诗歌中对此有过描写。

［18］当时的风俗为圣诞节前一天实行戒斋。

［19］虚拟地名。

［20］指高文所得的吻有所增加。

［21］列那，指狐狸。

［22］即向导。